T0369526

PETER REITZ

the
TRAP

iUniverse, Inc.
Bloomington

The Trap

iUniverse books may be ordered through booksellers or by contacting:

iUniverse
1663 Liberty Drive
Bloomington, IN 47403
www.iuniverse.com
1-800-Authors (1-800-288-4677)

ISBN: 978-1-4759-3223-2 (sc)
ISBN: 978-1-4759-3224-9 (e)
ISBN: 978-1-4759-3225-6 (hc)

Printed in the United States of America

iUniverse rev. date: 06/06/2012

DECEMBER 2011

Wilma and Robert Baldwin were the parents of two sons. Jack, the older son, was very conscientious and took care of his younger brother as much as he could. This responsibility was a daunting task. Hank, the younger son, was drawn to reprehensible behavior, and his mother, with sometimes-terrible consequences, spoiled him to the core, always minimizing his bad behavior and making excuses for him.

The Baldwin's ran a small family business, a poultry store, which required a lot of time and labor. Mrs. Baldwin always came to the store in the afternoon, when the store was really busy, and took care of the front counter.

One day, the phone rang, and Mrs. Baldwin answered, expecting another order. She politely said, "Poultry Barn, may I help you?"

The voice said, "This is Sergeant Peterson, Los Angeles Police Department. I need to speak to Mr. or Mrs. Baldwin."

"I'm Mrs. Wilma Baldwin, is there a problem?"

The officer went on to tell Mrs. Baldwin that her son Hank was at the police station, and she needed to come in. As she hung up, she told her husband that she had to pick Hank up from school. She always covered up for his bad behavior.

At the station, she found out her son was caught smoking marijuana. He had $824 in cash on him, and he had in his possession four packets of cocaine for sale, and rode a stolen bike. The policeman shook his head and told her how serious these crimes are, and that if Hank had been an adult, the punishment

1

would be severe. "Mrs. Baldwin, your son is just a young boy. If you don't nip this in the bud now, he might spend most of his life incarcerated. We have a big problem here."

Mrs. Baldwin responded, "I fully understand, and I'll take care of it."

I wonder who put him up to this she mumbled to herself, minimizing Hank's guilt as always. This incident was costing the Baldwin family many headaches, and would in the future. So far, she was able to keep this problem a secret from the family.

Leaving their two teenagers to their own devices after school seemed a little irresponsible. However, Jack was old enough and a very responsible young man. He picked his brother up from school, helped him with his homework, and they both had practice twice a week at the local park. The parents decided the year before to sign the boys up to participate in their favorite sports. Jack signed up for baseball, and Hank loved to play soccer. As it turned out, the boys were quite athletic and rapidly turned into excellent players in their chosen sports. Jack was the star of his team. To all the other teams he was known as "the pitcher from hell," because his pitching was super, and it frustrated most batters. On the other hand, Hank's soccer team featured a mixed bag of tricks. Sometimes they won against the best team in their league, but the next time only half the soccer team would show up.

During school, playing sports kept the boys busy and away from mischief. Unfortunately, during summer vacation the sports teams didn't play or practice, or start their seasons again until the start of school, leaving a two-month void. Jack and Hank's parents realized that their only option was for Mrs. Baldwin to stay home to take care of their boys; and having to hire a person to take over for Mrs. Baldwin became a burden on their financial condition.

The Baldwin's' poultry store was unique in that it provided live poultry in cages. People came to pick their fowl, and had their choices butchered and prepared while they were waiting. Their slogan advertised that they sold the freshest poultry in the city. Their customer base was mostly gourmet restaurants and people of means with exquisite taste. The work was physically demanding, and took its toll on Mr. Baldwin's health.

Mrs. Baldwin was busy with the boys. Games and practice, school activities, and running the household left her very little time to help in the store. Before they had children, the couple worked together in the store, and their income was substantially higher. As the boys grew older and more independent, Mrs. Baldwin was able to help the business. Sometimes even their sons had to help. Their financial situation improved by the time the boys were ready for college. The funds for their education were secure, and Jack, because of his academic achievements and talent in baseball, was offered a full scholarship from a prestigious university.

A year later, Hank was old enough to climb the ladder of higher learning. He was a talented soccer player, but his grades were merely average. In his second year, his grades took a downhill dive, and his interest in sports faded. He obviously picked the wrong crowd for his friends and became a party animal. The young man was wasting his time in school, and the financial resources of the family.

Drinking, driving, and wrecking a few cars while under the influence brought Hank a stint in county jail. In addition, rumors swirled around those two young women were pregnant, and Hank was suspected of being the father. He was totally out of control, but there was hope that by the end of his sentence he would become wiser and more considerate, and thereafter keep a good distance between himself and drugs.

Meanwhile, Jack completed his education and came home with a degree in business administration. He also had several job offers right away. He wound up managing a national trucking company. Jack was very well-liked. He received several promotions, a six-figure salary, became the trucking company's president, and took the company to new heights.

Jack also advised his father on business matters. The two men decided to expand, so Robert wouldn't have to work so hard physically. They took out loans including one of two hundred thousand dollars, and opened two new stores. Everything in the business went well, but Robert's health was failing. His struggles with lymphoma and diabetes took a heavy toll on him.

Soon Robert passed on, and Jack was forced to change course. He resigned from the trucking firm and took over the family's operation. Their loans needed to be paid back, and Jack knew his mother couldn't do it alone. Thanks to Jack's practical business understanding, the enterprise was financially in good shape. The business loans were paid off in the first season. The new stores did very well; whatever Jack touched turned into gold.

In the meantime, Wilma Baldwin pleaded with Jack every day to invite his brother in, to make it a real family business. Hank still had several weeks of incarceration to go. Finally, after daily nagging, and out of love for his mother, Jack caved in and invited Hank to join them in the family operation. Hank promised to put his heart and soul into it, and that he was through with partying. Their mother was happy that her baby boy was back in the family. She probably felt guilty, because she was the one that spoiled him, always making excuses for his behavior.

The business was running very well, and they accumulated a substantial profit. To take advantage of the surplus, Jack started to inquire about income properties. He was thinking of acquiring some apartment buildings, or possibly a strip mall or commercial office space. But fate took them in a much different direction.

The opportunity was a 120-acre cattle ranch in the Imperial Valley owned by a bank that held some business loans to Poultry Barn. Jack researched the deal and found it to be a good investment. They made an offer, and soon were the proud owners of a cattle ranch, but in the Imperial Valley running a cattle ranch consists mainly of growing alfalfa and feeding it to the stock. Actually, the land was more suitable for growing vegetables, and much more valuable than what they paid for it. They sold a hundred acres and doubled their investment. They used the twenty acres they still owned to raise their own poultry in order to keep prices down and stay competitive.

The plan was for Hank to run the farm, raising chickens, ducks, geese, and Cornish game hens; also to keep him away from the daily operation of the business, since he wasn't good dealing with people. Wilma loved the serenity of the ranch, so they planned to build a house for her and one for Hank. They built all outbuildings and cages at the same time. As soon as everything was ready, Wilma and Hank moved to Imperial Valley.

They hired two farmhands and started a breeding program. Because they raised more than they needed for the three stores, Jack found a connection with a local food chain. That company agreed to buy all the overflow the Poultry Barn could deliver, and expressed interest in receiving larger quantities in the future. To accommodate the demand, they had to build another brood house, buy two new trucks, and hire more people. The farm did well while Hank became a very good rancher. He took his position seriously, and raised more fowl then they ever expected.

Hank living on the farm together with Wilma made both of them very happy. Hank took excellent care of his ailing mother, but Wilma's health condition reached the end of the line, and she faded away peacefully. Thereafter, Hank suffered from depression, missing his mother terribly. The two of them, living on the farm together, were very fond of each other. Enjoying his mother's advice and guidance, he became a better man. During that period he didn't go out very much, took really good care of Wilma, and enjoyed her company. Once she was gone, he felt abandoned and lonely.

Soon thereafter, Hank's drinking started, and his outings to the local bar scene became frequent. He met all the local boozers, prostitutes, and dope peddlers. He threw money around in bars that caught the eye of dope dealers. It didn't take very long for him to become part of this drug scene. This conduct went on for quite a while, until one morning he woke up and found himself in his pickup on his friend Vic Carver's ranch. Upon talking to his friend, he found out how lucky he had been the night before. All the people in the cantina where arrested, including the owners of the bar. Hank happened to be so out of it earlier in the evening that in his stupor, he climbed into his truck to sleep it off. Vic, his friend and neighbor, came late to the cantina and realized what was happening. He jumped in Hank's truck and drove home, avoiding the bad scene of being arrested and the consequences thereof. Later on, a story in the local paper confirmed the ugly reality, that the cantina was shut down and most of the people arrested that night received sentences from six months to four years. Therefore, the party going on there was over for a while.

Hank and Vic became close friends, spending a lot of their free time together. Vic owned 140 acres of oranges, and his hobby was raising homing pigeons. Vic lost his wife four years earlier in an automobile accident. When his wife was alive, they belonged to a club with whom the

Frequently drove a truck loaded with homing pigeons hundreds of miles away and timed them to see how fast they would come home. The fastest fliers could win money and prizes, and therefore were more valuable to their owners.

Hank was fascinated with the homing pigeons and got an idea right away about how he could enroll them in the service of his new interest. "Since these pigeons used to carry mail, there's no reason why they can't carry a little cocaine from Mexico," said Hank.

"Don't be stupid," said Vic. "You can't send these pigeons to Mexico to pick up stuff."

"I know that, but hear me out.

"What we need is a connection with a poultry company that's willing to buy poultry from us. Even if we have to sell our birds very cheap, we make it up selling the junk. We take chicken and ducks and some homing pigeons across the border, sell the rest of the poultry, load our pigeons with dope and let them bring home the goods. 'Homing pigeons,' get it?"

Vic couldn't believe what he was hearing. "I hear you Hank, but I don't believe it. Can you repeat that?" he said.

"It's not that complicated," said Hank. "We need a truck with open cages that customs can see through so they'll have no doubt about our cargo. Once we get to our contact, we unload the chickens, ducks, geese, and game hens. Then we prep and load up the pigeons and let them fly, but not all at the same time. Since the distance isn't very far, they should be back within a few hours."

Vic listened skeptically and evaluated every point. "For a minute, I almost believed you were serious," he said.

"I am serious. Cocaine is very easy to put in little packets and tape to their legs. It won't diminish their capacity to fly."

For a while, Vic considered the plan, then agreed to try it out, thinking that it was something of a passing phase. At that time, Vic didn't know how stubborn Hank could be at times.

This business was between Hank and Vic only. They understood that their scheme had to be kept top secret. All telltale items had to be kept on Vic's property. Vic had some connections in La Quinta with a body shop owner named Toni, where he could order the custom truck with the cages, exactly the way they needed them.

Meanwhile, Hank took a trip across the border to establish a connection. He knew some people from his college days, but not well enough to trust them with such a proposition. Besides the one friend he was thinking about, was a lawyer in Guadalajara named Felix Mateo—a long way from Mexicali. He decided to scour the town of Mexicali, winding up in a butcher shop owned by a man named Carlos. He introduced himself to the owner and found out that he spoke perfect English, and that he lived in the US for twelve years. After a little small talk, Hank and Carlos started discussing business. Hank pointed out that Carlos could reduce his cost considerably.

"Show me your invoices off your purchases and I'll cut your price fifty percent. How does that sound?"

"Sounds great!" Carlos said "How can you sell your poultry so cheap?"

Hank told him without hesitation that he gets the feed from the US government very cheaply through a subsidy, and that they wouldn't like it if they found out he was selling his poultry in Mexico. In addition, to keep the Internal Revenue out of the picture, all transactions had to be in cash. Carlos the butcher seemed to understand the deal, so Hank and Carlos shook hands. As Hank was leaving, he turned around and informed Carlos that they could bring in the first shipment within ten days.

Carlos said, "That's fine, amigo. I'll be here!"

Hank got in his truck and drove off to look around the neighborhood, in order to get familiar with the area. He spotted a place called Cantina Temblor that looked interesting, so cruised around the block to find parking. From the parking spot on the way to the cantina, a whole block and a half, Hank took a good look at all the stores, and noticed some characters of lesser quality hanging about; the sort that always attracted Hank's attention.

Walking through the front door of the Temblor felt to him like coming home. Sitting down at the bar, he ordered a beer and started a conversation with the bartender. "My name's Hank. What's your name?"

People call me "Gordo, because I am *fat*," the barkeep answered, still facing the back of the bar.

There were only three people in the bar, and one was about to leave. The man at the end of the bar got up and said, "Adios, amigo."

Not turning around, the barkeeper answered, "Adios," observing everything in the mirrored shelves behind the bar.

Finally, Hank asked Gordo what he was hiding. He said to Hank, "When you walked in here, I recognized you immediately. You're Hank Baldwin. Are you with law enforcement, Hank?"

Hank said, "No."

"Are you with the law?"

As Hank shook his head, Gordo turned around.

"Francisco, you son of a bitch, how did you get out?" Hank said. Francisco the fat man responded

"It's a long story, amigo. The less you know, the better our friendship will be."

"Last time I saw you said Hank at Canyon Country with your friend the Sheriff of Los Angeles County."

"That's right; I got out a little earlier than expected."

"How? Did the laundry truck leave with you in it, a little early?"

"Something like that."

"It's good to see you again," said Hank.

"Same here," said Gordo, and shook hands over the counter. "I'm hiding here in Mexico. What are you doing here?"

"I'm in the poultry business, and I have a customer a few blocks away."

"Are you selling chicken to the supermarket?" Gordo asked.

Hank said, "No, I have business with Carlos the butcher."

Francisco said, "I know Carlos. From a small butcher shop he built his business into a successful supermarket. As a matter of fact, he has two markets. No need to call him Carlos the butcher anymore. Hank, you saw him in the little shop where he started many years ago. This will be a good connection for you. The man is very successful."

"I hope so," said Hank. After regurgitating their shady past for over an hour, it was time to go. "See you Francisco, the next time I'm in town."

"Adios, amigo," said Francisco.

On the way to his truck, Hank looked at all the stores and buildings to see if there was something for rent or for sale. They were in need of a warehouse where they could prep their pigeons. He needed a place that they could drive into and keep their activity from prying eyes. Hank also understood that they needed privacy when they released their flock. Therefore, he decided to drive out of town to check out availability. It looked hopeless. There wasn't a single property for sale or rent, so Hank decided to turn around and drive east; maybe the other direction would produce results. He went through town and out the other side. He had driven about forty-six miles when he spotted a stand of trees in the distance. As he got closer, he saw that it was an old citrus orchard, possibility suitable for his needs, so he approached it to investigate. As he approached the first structure, two Dobermans came to greet him. They didn't seem to be very friendly. He stayed in the truck, observing the dogs that were trying to get a hold of him.

Suddenly, he felt a cold pistol to his neck. A chill went down his spine. The person behind the pistol spoke something in Spanish in a low voice. Hank screamed, "Amigo, don't shoot!" as a woman approached the truck from the front.

Stopping about five feet from the truck, she asked in plain English, "What do you want?"

Hank said, "I'm a farmer, and I'm looking for some land."

"What kind of farmer are you? This is just a small family farm. It's hardly a place to farm and expect to profit."

"Actually, I'm not a farmer in the sense that you think. I'm in the poultry business."

She said, "What is poultry business?"

"Chickens, ducks, geese; you know: *pollos, patos* for food," Hank said.

"Oh, I see," she answered. "Stay in the truck. I'll put the dogs away."

"I hope so," said Hank. "They scare me."

After she put the dogs away, Hank stepped out of the truck. When Hank turned around, he was amazed to see the person that held the gun was an older woman. She disguised her voice, so the stranger would think that it was a man behind the gun.

The younger woman came back and asked him to come in to the house. It was a very hot day; they needed to get out of the sun. In the house, Hank revealed his name and told the women he meant no harm. The older one still held the gun, not pointing at him, but still suspicious. Hank asked, "Why you are here alone; where are the men?"

"They should be back very soon. They went into town to buy supplies," the young woman replied, then said, "My name is Miranda and this is my mother. Her name is Maria and our family name is Hernandez."

She offered him a glass of water and drank some herself. Her mother did still not trust the stranger. They made small talk, and after an hour and a half, she broke down and admitted that there was no one coming, with tears in her eyes. She told Hank that her father passed away the month before, and she had to come back to take care of her mother. "I lived in the States, in Pasadena for six years, working in a nursery. I loved the job and I would like to go back there, but my mother doesn't want to abandon the farm. She says to me, if we leave the farm, all the trees will die that your father planted as a young man.

"Besides, I grew up here, just like the trees. She always took care of me, and the trees took care of us. She's very sentimental. I want to sell, but my mother will never agree. She's getting a little senile, worrying about these trees, as if they were my siblings. I grew up here, but I must say it was a lonely life, now that I have seen and experienced city life."

Hank told her, "I know how this loneliness feels, because I live on a ranch in the Imperial Valley, on the other side of the border."

"In that case, you understand," Miranda said. "If I have to live here, I'll die before my mother. When you live in an isolated place after some time away from that loneliness, the feeling is depressing, even though I grew up here. I need to convince her that there is no other way but to sell the orchard. We could probably get twenty-five thousand dollars for the ranch. That would give us a nice start in the States."

Hank's wheels were turning. He turned on his charm and began telling Miranda that he would like to buy the farm and would always take good care of the trees. Miranda translated this proposal to her mother, but as soon as she heard that Hank offered to buy the farm, she started crying. Hank jumped in the conversation and reassured her that he would keep his promise. Maria told her daughter that she realized that they couldn't stay. She still didn't trust Hank, but was willing to agree to sell once she had the cash in her hands. Hank shook hands with both women. Miranda was smiling from ear to ear, but Maria was still skeptical. As he was saying good-bye, he told them that he would come back in a few days to finalize the deal and bring the money.

So Hank had accomplished what he set out to do. His mind wandered from the butcher shop to the cantina and the women at the ranch. He had a satisfied smirk on his face approaching the border on his way home, as he drove straight to Vic's place. Enthusiastically, he told the story, describing every detail, and declared a time for celebration. Vic was happy too, and agreed to do something fun.

Vic lost his wife four years earlier in an automobile accident and was longing for some female company. Hank suggested that they go to see some women he knew at the Salton Sea. On the way, Hank told Vic that most of the people who hung out there were running from something, always looking for opportunities to take advantage of other people. "So do don't reveal anything to them or it will come back to haunt you," Hank warned.

Vic replied, "We fit right in. Isn't that what we're doing?"

"I guess so," Hank replied. "But as far as they are concerned, we're just two farm boys looking for a good time."

The Salton Sea was created between 1905 and 1907 by a faulty irrigation control canal. The area is a cauldron much lower than sea level that filled up with Colorado River water. The lake is approximately fifteen miles wide and thirty miles long. Being only thirty miles south of Palm Springs, it became a convenient oasis in the desert and a playground for the Hollywood elite. With boating, fishing, and water skiing in the hot desert sun, Salton Sea was the perfect holiday destination. Yacht clubs, hotels, and motels sprang up around the lake. What seemed to be too good to be true was in fact just that. Its popularity in the fifties and sixties went into decline, because its salinity increased so much that some species of fish started dying out in parts of the lake. Slowly, the communities around the lake declined to attract tourists. Water levels started to increase. Property owners had to retreat, building makeshift marinas and creating all sorts of Band-Aid fixes. Most places went downhill fast. Buildings and houses were abandoned, and riffraff started moving in.

There was a small colony of prostitutes on the west side. Hank and Vic aimed straight for the place the two men referred to as Hookerville at seventy-five miles per hour. The sign on the place said Mabel's Market. Vic asked Hank if he needed some groceries, and Vic replied no, the market that was just a front.

"Hank! There's a sheriff coming out of the place," Vic said, turning pale.

"Ignore him. Let's just walk toward the lake," Hank replied.

As they passed the first house, a woman said, "Hello, boys."

Hank replied, "A sheriff just walked out of the store."

She said, "Don't worry, gentlemen. He's just a customer, usually twice a week, and he always walks out through the store with a bag of chips or beef jerky that Mabel hands him on the way out. You boys came for some loving?"

Before the men could answer, she said, "Oh, by the way, my name is Sue and I run this place. There are three girls in the next house and two more in the house on the right side. You can have your pick. It's 120 bucks apiece. Since I run the joint, I pick for you, and if you're very kinky, you have to wait for an hour because Sadie is busy right now.

"Before we do anything, you hand me the money for safekeeping, emphasis on keeping! And if you're okay with that, come in the kitchen and buy Sue a beer and a shot. If you people are thirsty I have everything in here."

The men stepped inside the house and sat down around the kitchen table. Sue asked them what they wanted, and Vic answered, "Just a beer for me please," and Hank just nodded. She served the beers and poured herself a double shot of Jack Daniels, then went on the phone.

"We have company," she said. "There are two gentlemen who would like to see you."

She hung up and sat down with us at the table. In less than ten minutes two women showed up. Sue got up and said, "Let me introduce you. This is Betty, and this is Trixy. The guys are Bob and Frank."

The guys looked at each other, and Vic was about to say, "We are," when Trixie said, "We know, but we don't care. Yesterday I was Roberta; today I'm Trixie, and tomorrow, who knows?"

Betty asked for a beer. Trixie wanted a glass of wine. Sue brought out the drinks, put them on the table, and said, "Cheers!" and all took a drink.

"Three hundred bucks should cover it," said Sue, as she stretched out her hand. Hank took out his wallet and gave Sue the money. She said, "Thanks, you're good to go."

The girls took them by their hands and walked them to the house in the back, winding up in different bedrooms. The perfumed air and anticipation of the encounter with the ladies was exciting for the men. Since it had been a while for both men, the time spent with the women was short and sweet. They were out in twenty-five minutes, thanking the girls, and off they went. Walking by the front house, they waved good-bye to Sue, climbed into the truck, and took off.

Neither one said a word on the way home, as if coming home from a funeral. Hank dropped Vic off at his place. As he stepped out of the truck, he lifted his arm halfway and went in the house. Hank turned around and went home to get some sleep.

The next morning, Hank drove over to Vic s place to plan their next move. They talked about the previous night, the fun with the girls, and of course, razzed each other about the short time they spent with the women last night.

After a couple of cups of coffee, Hank suggested making a trial run. "Let's take a dozen homers," as he called them, "and put them on my pickup in that green wire cage over there. I'll take them across the border into Mexico and let them go. We'll time them so we know how long it takes them to return."

"We also need to figure out how much weight they can take. So far, they've only carried little notes attached to their feet," said Vic.

"Well, let's try it out. Get a couple of birds, and we'll attach some weight to their legs to see how they're doing. How are we going to attach the weights?

"For now, let's just tape them on. I have some small weights in my tackle box, there on the top shelf," Vic said.

"These are probably too big," Hank sighed, shaking his head.

"I have some the size of a pea, the kind you pinch on the fishing line," Vic suggested.

"That's great, go get the birds."

Hank went into Vic's office to fetch the tape. Vic came back with six pigeons, and the guys started to prep them.

Vic said, "I'm going to get the postal scale. Otherwise, we won't know how much they can handle. Let's put half an ounce on the first one, three quarters of an ounce on the second one, and a full ounce on the third."

"Yes, we need to repeat that on the next three birds," said Hank.

"And put them back in the shed," Vic followed.

Usually, Vic would open three cages at a time and let them fly for their exercise. This time he opened only two. The birds went up in circles until they could barely see them. The circles got bigger until they could no longer see them. After thirty-five minutes, the flock returned. It was a beautiful sight to watch twenty-four birds coming home and landing on their perches.

Vic said, "Tomorrow, when you go to Mexico, take twenty-four birds, different ones, and stop at the hardware store. Or better yet, stop at the tackle shop and pick up enough weights. When you get to Mexico and get them all prepped, call me, so I can time them. Put the weights on half of them. Then let them all go together."

"Okay," said Hank. "Meanwhile, Vic, you should go to the bank and get a twenty-five thousand dollar cashier's check made out to Maria Hernandez. Maybe on the next trip I can seal the deal with Miranda and Maria.."

"I think you'd better get in touch with a lawyer in Mexico to advise you about all the legalities about Mexican real estate law," said Vic.

"I'll see what I can do."

Hank got on his way to Mexicali. He made sure that everything was in order so there would be no trouble with Mexican border patrol. Usually they just say, "Welcome to Mexico."

After crossing the border, Hank drove through town to the vicinity of the ladies' ranch, pulled off the road, and started prepping the pigeons. He had to take them into the truck's cab so they couldn't fly away. After he was ready, he took out his cell phone and called Vic to tell him that everything was okay and that he was ready to open the cages. Then he said, "Wait a minute, there's a slow-moving truck driving by. I might have to wait or move to another location."

"All right, be careful," said Vic.

"I'm starting the truck and I'll be moving further away from the road."

After five minutes, Hank called Vic again and said, "I'm in a secure location. I'm letting the birds go. It's now five minutes after three. I'll see you at home."

Hank had an uneventful trip home. When he arrived, the pigeons were already there, all twenty-four of them—good news indeed.

Vic said, "I'll have to pick up the truck tomorrow. Tony called me a while ago to say that the painter just finished the sign on the truck, and it looks good. You better get on the stick with that lawyer friend of yours in Mexico."

"All right, I'll give him a call right now."

Reaching for his cell phone, Hank realized he didn't have the number of his former classmate Felix Mateo, or five or six other names he couldn't remember anymore. "I'm sure I have his phone number in my office, so I'll see you later. I'll let you know what he said."

"Okay," said Vic, and went into the house. Hank waved and drove off.

In his office, Hank looked in his phone book and typed in the number. A woman answered in Spanish. He asked for Felix.

Hank and Felix reminisced about their party days in school, the wild nights, and in somber days, smoking pot and missing classes. And the girls. "Do you remember Pat Wilson? She was always willing. And Mary Hamilton," Hank said.

"Yeah, and her too," replied Felix. After a long pause, Felix mumbled, "Mary is my wife now."

After another pause, Hank replied, "Congratulations, Felix, and give my regards to Mary."

Following another pause, Felix said, "Just send me the papers. I'll look through them and will call you."

"Very well. Thanks a lot, Felix; I'll talk to you soon. Good-bye."

"Yeah," Felix replied.

They both felt awkward, because on their highs they sometimes exchanged partners; and Felix married one of them. Of course, there were other girls, and for Felix there was a cloud of suspicion that ripped through his being. That Hank might be the father of Hank junior Even Hank felt awkward, even though he did not know about the boy .Normally not much bothered him. But this surprise threw him for a loop when Felix's voice turned into a chill for Hank.

Hank sat in his office with his feet on the desk, leaned back in his chair, and mentally went back to that time span in school. He saw Mary with understanding eyes, caressing her cheeks, stroking her hair, hugging her gently, and apologizing with tears in his eyes. The door opened suddenly, and his foreman walked in, saying, "You wanted to see me Chief?" They all called him Chief ever since they had a little fire in the feed barn and Hank grabbed the hose and put the fire out. There was sarcasm galore in this outfit, but when Diego saw his face with tears in his eyes, he asked if there was anything he could do.

Hank said, "Do what? Wash the sand out? I got some crap in my face out there." The reason I wanted to see you—I sold fifty chickens and ten ducks to a guy in town. Put them in cages, and load them on my pickup. I'll take them in the morning."

"Okay, Chief."

"Thanks, Diego. I'll see you in the morning."

Hank sat back in his chair and rejoined Mary in his mind. He was in love with Mary and didn't realize it before; now he was hurting. He always felt there was something missing, and now he thought he knew what it was.

When Diego came back in the morning and saw Hank was still in his chair, he gently closed the door again, went outside to the pickup, and honked the horn. Hank jumped up, opened the door, and asked Diego, "What's going on?"

Diego said, "Sorry, I leaned against the horn, Chief. It's okay; I was just daydreaming," and the noise startled me replied hank.

Hank put his hat on, rubbed his eyes, and walked to his house to shower and clean up. Feeling a little better and having coffee with the boys in the office, he even joked around. He told them he was drinking and fell asleep in the chair. But he realized that they knew that he was in the chair all night.

After their coffee social, Hank got in the truck and drove to Vic's place to discuss with him the trip across the border and to prep the invoices for the butcher's first delivery.

"Make sure you let them know at the border that you will have deliveries on weekly basis," Vic advised.

After Vic handed him the invoices, Hank glanced at them and did a double take. "You're kidding! You called us Airborne Poultry

Company. Are you out of your freaking mind? Isn't that a little obvious?"

"No that's just it; nobody will even think about it. You do because you know it."

"I hope you're right."

"We have it on the truck, too, so get used to it."

Hank jumped in his truck and headed south. He encountered no problem at the border, and kept on going to the butcher to deliver his load. Hank called Carlos to tell him he was on his way, and that he would meet him at the shop. When Hank arrived, Carlos waved Hank to the back of the shop, where all the cages were.

"Hello, amigo," he said. "Very nice chickens and these ducks look good too, but you only brought fifty today. I need double that twice a week at least. You don't have the means to raise more poultry."

"I do, but the cheap feed I get from the government is limited. If you need more, the price is going up thirty percent."

"Ouch," said Carlos.

Hank was quick to add, "You're still twenty percent ahead."

"They're very healthy birds," said Carlos.

"They're very nice. And why didn't you tell me that you own the big supermarket? You let me think you're just a small butcher shop owner."

"You never asked, and I'm not one to brag. I also own a market in Tijuana, and this shop here prepares the poultry for both stores."

The two men went in the office where Carlos handed Hank the cash. Hank thanked him and told him that he needed time to increase his capacity.

After saying their good-byes, Hank got on his way to see Miranda and her mother about the orchard and encountered the same greeting; the two Dobermans were anxious to tear Hank apart. Miranda came out right away to fetch the dogs. Maria opened the door, and waved Hank in.

After putting the dogs away, Miranda came in the back door. "How are you?" she said.

"I'm well. How is everything going here?"

"Very well. I went to Tecate yesterday to see my uncle. He's a bookkeeper, and he told me what papers I need to sell the farm. He was nice to come by last night with the documents and helped me fill them out."

"That's great," said Hank. "I'll make copies of them and bring the money tomorrow. We'll go to a local attorney together and finalize the deal."

"Very good," said Miranda.

"All right, tomorrow then. Adios, Maria; and good-bye Miranda."

Maria smiled a little as Hank closed the door. Hank drove straight home and tried to call Felix to advise him on the paperwork.

He punched in the number, and a female voice answered again: *Hola*, and some other words in Spanish. Hank recognized Mary's voice immediately. He experienced a hot flash through his whole body, and in a crackled voice he said, "Hello, Mary."

"Oh my God!" said Mary. "H-Hank, is that you?"

Hank answered, "Yes, it's so good to hear your voice."

Mary started to weep. In a broken voice she said, "How are you Hank?" He replied that he was okay. Mary went on to say that Felix is very controlling and jealous and that she couldn't take it anymore.

"He knows that my son isn't his, and he aims to destroy me. He's a bitter man."

"Mary, I'm so sorry we lost touch. You remember the drinking and partying, but I always loved you, and I do even more so now. Whenever you want to talk, here is my cell number."

She wrote down the number and started to speak in Spanish. Hank realized that meant she couldn't talk anymore, so he hung up.

He stared at the window for a while, thinking about Mary.

Then he picked up the phone and called Vic. He told him all the things that were going on that day and that he had the papers for the orchard. Hank told him that in the morning he would drive over there to finalize the deal. Then Hank said, "I guess I'll see you in the morning."

Victor detected sadness in Hank's voice, and said, "Wait a minute, what's the matter?"

"Nothing, I'm just tired, that's all."

"Just hang on a minute. I'll bring you the cashier's check for the orchard, so you don't have to stop by in the morning, and you can leave early. I'll be busy tomorrow anyway. I hired some laborers to come and weed the orchard."

Ten minutes later, Vic showed up at Hank's house. "How do you feel? You sounded pathetic on the phone; what's the matter?"

Hank told him the story. Vic said, "This really is great! That's good news. Why are you so down on yourself?"

Hank said, "I don't know what to do. Mary sounded so unhappy. She cried. I just don't know what to do. I'm so in love with her that it hurts."

Vic tried to cheer him up and joked about it, complaining that he might have to take care of all those women at the lake by himself. "Not fair, not fair at all," he said.

Hank cracked a smile and said, "I feel so sorry for you, Speedy!"

"It didn't take you very long either, so don't call the kettle black, when you're the stove."

"But seriously, what should I do? She had no time to tell me what she had in mind. Apparently someone walked in on her, so she started speaking Spanish."

Vic said, "The only thing you can do is to wait for her call. Make sure your cell phone is charged all the time so you don't miss her call. I'm sure it won't be too long if she's that miserable and unhappy. Go get some sleep and I'll see you tomorrow afternoon. Good night."

Hank finally got a good night's sleep and felt much better in the morning. After he had some coffee with the boys again, he got in his truck and headed south once more. He kept his cell phone in his shirt pocket, anxiously hoping for Mary's call.

At the border he befriended several people, so he stopped to say hello. He told them that he had to take care of some paperwork in Mexicali and would be back in the afternoon. Off he went to pick up Miranda and her mother to take them with him to a lawyer.

After he turned into the ranch and the ladies took care of the dogs, they were ready to get down to business. "Good morning," said Hank. "Did you find a lawyer?"

Miranda answered, "Yes, I called him. His office is right by the courthouse about forty minutes from here."

"Great. So how are you today?"

She said, "Well, my mom is a little sad. She got up early this morning and walked slowly through the orchard. I think she was saying good-bye to each and every tree. I had tears in my eyes when I saw that, but things have to be done that we don't like sometimes. And this is one of them.

"I called my former employer, and he'll be happy to have me back, so after we take care of the papers, I'll go to Pasadena to try to find an apartment—if my old apartment is rented already by someone else."

"Good luck with that," Hank said, "And here's the courthouse."

"Oh yes." she said. "His office is in the back. His name is Abel Lopez, and he's expecting us. The fees are a hundred and eighty dollars."

"Fine, "said Hank. "Let's go in. Watch your step. The courtyard is nice. Look at the bougainvillea's in full bloom."

"Yes, very lovely," said Miranda. Her mom just stood there and looked with a smile. She loved flowers and all of Mother Nature's creations.

After twenty minutes or so, they were done with the papers, and Hank took the ladies back to the ranch. They all went in the house, Hank had a beer, took a look around, and then they took a walk through the orchard while Miranda explained to Hank how their watering system worked.

"In three weeks, everything is going to be complete. When you get back from Pasadena and the papers are done, call me and I'll come to pick them up," Hank said.

"I will," she said. Then they walked to the front. Maria was standing there by his truck. He hugged her and then Miranda, and got in his truck.

He drove straight home, because he had a lot of paperwork to do at the ranch. His brother reminded him to send the quarterly statements to the main office. He worked all afternoon and the next morning, and finally sent it in, then went to see Vic.

They were just having lunch, so Hank joined them. One of the men that did the weeding barbecued some porterhouse that Vic had in his freezer. They also had a bunch of corn on the barbecue, and a big watermelon. "Not a bad lunch," Hank commented.

After lunch, Hank asked where the new truck was, and Vic said it was in the barn. "Let's go and look at it," said Hank. When he saw it, he commented, "Very flashy! Everyone from here to Mexicali is going to notice this truck."

"That's the whole idea. No one will think that anyone would be so stupid as to haul junk in this flashy rig. And actually, we won't haul anything illegal; but people are going to be more inclined to trust us because of this truck."

"I guess so. By the way, in about two weeks, we'll get the papers for the ranch in Mexico. I took a look around today, and I must say it's a nice ten-acre orchard. The trees look good and the outbuildings are totally usable. As I see it," Hank said, "we need to build a brooding house and cages on your property as soon as possible."

Vic agreed. "If your brother were ever to show up unexpectedly, we'd have a big problem, right?"

After a pause, Hank said he didn't hear what Vic said. Vic asked, "Where are you, thinking of Mary again?"

Hank said, "I just don't know why she didn't call. Maybe I've read too much into it; maybe she was just complaining, or maybe Felix is abusive to her, or ..."

Vic snapped at him, "Since when did you become the king of maybe? I'm sure she's going to call whenever she's ready, so snap out of it. You're Hank Baldwin. We have to concentrate on our project."

"You're right, Vic. I'll see you tomorrow."

As he was driving, his mind wondered again about Mary and her predicament, and also about feeling sorry for himself. He got home to take care of some chores and went to bed. He didn't get much sleep, but he got up early in the morning, drove down to Mexicali to deliver his load, and collected the money. He was already back by ten thirty. He went into his house and took a nap. At two thirty he woke up, took a shower, and went over to Vic's place to see what was going on.

Vic informed him that he ordered the cages, and the guys were coming in the morning to install them. "The brooding set is just like yours."

"That's good said Hank so there's no learning period.

Hank had a story to tell and an idea. "Listen, I watched a show last night that was fascinating. There was a guy that had a nest of wild geese on the side of his pond in the grass under a bush. As he took an evening stroll with his dogs, they surprised the geese, and by the time he called them off, the goose was dead and the gander was in bad shape. He took the gander in the house and tried to patch him up and put him in a box. Then he went looking for the babies. He brought all eight goslings in and put them in the box with their father. In the morning, the gander was dead.

"The farmer, feeling guilty because his dogs wiped out the parents of the goslings, became Mother Goose. The man took the goslings out every day, so they could eat grass and swim in the pond. He also supplemented their diets with boiled corn. They followed him everywhere. One day he got in his car and drove off to Walmart. Without his noticing, the goslings flew behind him and also wound up in the parking lot of the store. He created quite a commotion. People started gathering around to watch this spectacle as the goslings surrounded him. He had no choice but to turn around and drive home. It was a beautiful sight to see a flock of geese flying twenty feet above the car. So from then on, his wife had to do all the shopping, at least until the goslings flew south for the winter.

"One Sunday morning, the farmer took his micro-light aircraft out of the barn. He prepped it to go on a flight, confidently thinking that this noisy machine would scare the goslings, and therefore they wouldn't follow him. When he took off, he didn't see them. He thought they were either on the pond or in the barn. But as soon as he was up in the air, the goslings joined him. After the amazement, he realized that he would have to take them out on a regular basis to get them in shape for the migration south in the fall.

"After a wonderful summer, the first flocks of migrating Canadian geese were spotted. Some landed in the cornfields, and some flocks were seen on the river, but the farmer's flock wasn't motivated to join them. The migration was almost over when the farmer decided he had no option but to lead them down south to the gulf with his aircraft—which he did. He spent a few days with them on a sandy beach, waiting for his friend to pick him and his aircraft up for the trip back home. They had to sneak off in the middle of the night, so the geese wouldn't follow them back home."

Vic said, "It's an interesting story, but what does it have to do with us?"

Hank explained, "Listen, these geese seem to be very clingy. What if we put them together with some homing pigeons so they could get used to their leadership and follow them? They could haul a lot more weight."

"Hank, you're a dreamer. If you want to spend the time to do all that, go ahead. In the meantime, let's concentrate on the pigeons. We don't even know if that works, so let's take one step at a time, otherwise we're going to trip."

"You're right. I'll try something later. I have to make another delivery on Friday. You think we should try some pigeons this trip?"

"Not yet, just in case there are some different customs agents at the border. You need their complete trust. Take chickens and bring some back, just so the border guards can see them on the American side. That way they get used to the chickens and all the rest of the poultry. If they ask you why you're bringing them back, just tell them the customer didn't need so many. That should be good enough. Did you ever get a connection to supply us with some junk?"

Hank said, "No, not yet. I think when I'm down there I'll stop by the cantina and talk to Gordo. I'll just ask him if he knows where to get some just for personal use. I don't trust him just yet."

Everything went smoothly at the border going in. Also, the delivery and transaction were handled by Carlos's foreman, an indication that Carlos trusted Hank, giving a boost to the reputation of his business.

On his way to the cantina, Hank looked around to see if there was some illegal activity going on. No luck, so he parked and went into the Cantina Temblor.

Francisco greeted him. "Hank, welcome. How are you?"

"I'm good, how are you Francisco?"

"I'm still *fat*. A cold one?"

"Yeah."

"How is this chicken business?"

In reply Hank said, "So far, it's developing very nicely. Hey, do you have a connection where I could get a little coke?"

"Maybe," Francisco said. "If you just need a little, I have an ounce here."

"That's great. I need it for my girlfriend. She likes a little boost once in a while, and I'm going to see her tonight."

"Good for you. Are you sure that's enough?"

"I'm sure I don't want to stay a whole week with her. Thanks, Francisco. I have to go. I still have some chickens on the truck, and I don't want them to die in the sun."

"Oh, I see. Adios amigo, see you soon."

When Hank got to the truck, to his surprise, all the chickens were gone. He looked around, but of course, no one saw anything. He was talking to himself, cussing up and down the scale from one to ten, scoring a nine. He got in the truck and took off. In the next block he threw out the cocaine he just purchased just in case Gordo had set him up. He went to the border and all the way home, puzzled by what happened.

Hank arrived at Vic's ranch and told him about his adventure in Mexicali, with the loss of the chickens and his new purchase of junk.

"Good move, better safe than sorry," said Vic. "Oh, come see; they're almost done with the cages, and tomorrow they'll finish the brood house."

"That's great," said Hank. "I have about two hundred fertile eggs we can use. I'll bring them over tomorrow and we can get started. That part I'm very familiar with, I've been doing this for a long time. I can teach you all you need to know about raising poultry."

"I'm excited," said Vic.

They started making weekly deliveries to Carlos, taking pigeons along to let them fly and timing them. The second week the number eighteen bird didn't come home, so Hank and Vic agreed to suspend the flights for a while until they figured out what happened. After two weeks they resumed the flights. Hank used a different location every time in case somebody was waiting for them when they flew over. The two were contemplating all possibilities.

Hank said, "Maybe we worry too much. After all, it could have been a hawk or a falcon, or even a golden eagle. Even if somebody shot her down, they wouldn't find evidence of illegal activity, and there's even less of a chance that the bird would lead them to us. But in the future, with a bird loaded with junk, it would be a different story. We have to make sure that every bird is photographed, and keep records of every flight and time. Let's try to put five slower fliers with the flock and put only weight on them. My theory is that if someone is shooting pigeons, and he spots the flock, by the time he's ready to shoot at them it would be the tail end of the flock, and the slow fliers with only weights on them would fall. We should even put a note on them with the address of the mansion of the mayor of Los Angeles, to throw them off. It would hit the papers and people would assume that the mayor is involved. The media would let us know right away, and then we could take precautions."

Vic was worried that with the birds coming home in daylight, people in the Valley could see them. "You know they don't fly at night."

Hank, of course, always had an answer for everything. He suggested, "Why don't we advertise in the paper that we have a little side business, meaning that we rent a flock of white pigeons to be released at weddings. And since they always come home, it would be no loss to us."

"There are not that many weddings in the Imperial Valley and adjacent communities," Vic objected.

"It doesn't matter. We could take them out on weekends and let them fly. That way people could see them and get used to them, and get interested in renting them for special occasions."

"Brilliant," said Vic. "You have a devious mind."

"If you need a quick answer, you're forced to think of something."

"Yes I know," said Vic, "but you always come up with the answer so quick it makes my head spin."

"If you need a spin, we have to go and see the ladies at the Salton Sea again."

"Yeah, maybe Friday night," Vic replied. "Maybe you can beat your speed record."

"Oh shut up, Vic. Shouldn't you get ready for tomorrow?"

"I guess so," Vic replied, and went into the pigeon coops to take care of some chores.

The week went by without any major complications. On Friday evening the guys got ready to visit the ladies.

Upon their arrival, Sue was at the window. Sue said, "Hello gentlemen, it's nice to see you again. Do come in. I have everything you want in here. It'll be the same routine as the last time: the drinks, the phone calls, and the ladies show up. Let me introduce you. This is Kelly and Laura, and this is Joe and Bruce."

They all smiled, and Hank said, "You see, Vic—you always get something different in this outfit."

"These are the same girls."

"Yeah, but today it's Laura and Kelly. Can't you see the difference?" They both laughed and went to the house in the back.

After routinely getting undressed and a little caressing, Hank's cell phone started to ring. He just ignored it for a while until it started to annoy him. Hank scrambled for his jeans to shut the phone down, but decided to check first who was bothering him. He thought it was his brother and answered the phone by saying, "What do you want, Jack?"

The answer came in Mary's voice, "Hello Hank, how are you?"

Hank answered, "I'm so sorry, I thought it was my brother trying to aggravate me, which he does from time to time. Never mind how I am. How are *you*? Can you talk where you are?"

There was a little pause, and Mary said, "I left Felix, and I'm in Ventura."

Hank asked, "Ventura, California?"

She said, "Yes, I'm at my parents' house."

"I want to see you," he said.

She answered, "I want to see you too."

"Mary, I want to see you tonight, I'll be there in four hours. Give me your cell phone number. I'll call you right back."

As he started to dress himself, Kelly, the woman entertaining Hank, who she called Joe, thought that Joe's wife was on her way over, and asked Joe if she's violent.

Hank laughed and said, "She isn't my wife. The lady I talked to is two hundred miles from here, so don't worry."

"You lied," she replied, "because you said that you will see her tonight."

"Yes, I'll see her in about four hours."

Kelly said, "This woman must be very special.

"She is and so are you. Thank you for the lovely time you shared with me." Hank got dressed and went to rouse Vic, alias Bruce.

Hank went across the hallway, knocked on the door, and said, "Bruce, we have to go, something came up."

With sarcasm, Vic replied, "Something is still up over here."

Hank knew that short visit would haunt him for a long time. He said, "I'll wait for you in the truck. Don't take too long. We really need to go. Now I feel stupid, telling you not to take too long."

After fifteen minutes, Vic showed up smiling, jumped in the truck, and started hassling Hank, calling him king of pop, speedball, and record holder, among other humiliating names. "Way to go, Joe," Vic said, calling him by the name that Sue gave him. "What's the problem?"

"Mary called while I was getting involved," Hank explained to Vic. "So I had to skip the whole thing."

"You're not the only one who lost concentration. After I talked to you; it just wasn't the same."

"Stop it already. I know I deserve the sarcasm. Listen, I told Mary I'd see her in four hours. She's with her parents in Ventura. I looked it up on my phone, and I reserved a room at the Pierpont Inn. And I told Mary to go there to room twenty-seven and wait for me. I can't wait to see her; I'm so excited."

Vic said, "Good for you," as he stepped out of the truck. "I'm sorry about the hassling, Hank. I'm really happy for you."

"Thank you, I'll call you tomorrow."

"Okay Hank. Good luck and good night."

Hank stopped at home to shower and clean up and pack clothes for the trip. As he was driving, he thought constantly about Mary, hoping that she would be madly in love with him, as he was in love with her. He was so anxious and impatient that he sped along the way, arriving at the Pierpont Inn at 2:38 a.m.

What a glorious reunion they experienced! The next day they slept in, and in the afternoon they went together to her parents' house to meet her family. When Hank saw Mary's son, Hank just stood there, seeing in him an image of himself as a young boy.

"Oh my God, you never told me that it was our son."

Mary said, "I'm sorry, I didn't want you to think that he was the reason that I called you. You know I love you and now you know you have a son."

"Mary, we have so much to catch up on. There won't be a boring day for the rest of our lives." So Hank turned to the boy and asked, "What is your name young man?"

He answered, "I'm not a man, and my name is Hank. And who are you?"

"I'm Hank Baldwin."

"You're the first Hank I ever met," said the boy—just like his father, a true Baldwin.

The next two days were the highlight of Mary and Hank's lives. The couple decided to get married. Hank had to go back to the ranch to take care of business, and Mary would take care of wedding plans. The arrangements would be simple and meaningful.

Hank called his brother to tell him the news. At first, Jack was apprehensive, thinking of Hank's track record and unreliability. But Hank explained that it wasn't a momentary decision, that he had been in love with Mary for twelve years, and that it had been his fault that his partying and drug use caused them to lose touch with each other. He also told Jack that Mary was the missing link in his life, and the super-bonus was his son. "He's turning ten in October—a Libra, just like me." Jack told Hank that he was happy for him and congratulated him. For Hank that was huge. He always sought his brother's approval, and this time he had it.

Back at the ranch, Hank had to catch up on some chores, make his deliveries, and check the brood houses to make sure the temperature settings were correct. Vic informed him that the Canadian geese eggs arrived and that they needed to be put in the brooder.

Vic said, "The deliveries for Carlos are all loaded and ready for you as soon as you are."

"I'll make the deliveries to Carlos in the morning, and in the afternoon I'll take care of the wild Canadian goose eggs."

"All right, then I'll see you in the afternoon."

After Hank arrived at the ranch, he took care of his chores and told Vic that he had much to tell him. They went into his house, and Hank told him all about Mary and his son. "You wouldn't believe it, Vic. He's just like I was at his age. Mary and I decided to get married, and she's working on the details. I also talked to my brother, and he seems to be happy for me, so all systems are go."

"Hank, I congratulate you and wish you the best."

"Thank you," Hank responded. "Let's open a bottle of wine and toast to my good fortune. I know you're going to like Mary too. She's something else."

"Cheers to you and Mary's happiness—oh yeah—and to Hank Jr."

At home, he got on the phone to talk to Mary about how plans were going. She told him how happy she was and that the wedding should be as simple as possible. She told Hank that when she got married to Felix it was a big, beautiful, over-the-top wedding in Guadalajara, and that such a beautiful, expensive wedding was the biggest disappointment of her life. "I know," she said, "it's not the wedding that made things so awful for me; it was Felix. But the reminder would be there, and I would like to avoid that."

"I understand how you feel," said Hank, "and I respect that. And personally, I'm not too comfortable in large groups. Whenever and wherever you decide is fine with me."

She replied, "I was at a wedding some time ago in the San Fernando Valley. As I recall, it was on Coldwater Canyon, not too far from Ventura Boulevard. The place is called the Little Brown Church. I think I would like to have our wedding there."

"It's your call Mary; whatever you decide is fine with me," said Hank.

"I want you to come to the ranch. Do you want me to pick you up, or can you borrow a car from your parents? If not, I'll call Enterprise Rent-A-Car, and they'll come and pick you up so you can drive out here."

"That would be nice. But Mom lets me drive her car." The next day, Mary started the trip south in her mother's car, stopping by at the Little Brown Church to make the arrangements. So then they had a date and the place to get married. All that was left was to invite some of their family and friends.

When she arrived at the ranch, Hank had a big smile on his face, and Mary was gloating too. Hank noticed she was alone in the car. "Where's Hank?" he asked right away. She explained that he couldn't pass up a fishing trip with Grandpa. "Yeah, I can see how I would lose out on that deal. Fishing is more fun than sitting in the car for three hours. Besides, he doesn't know me that well, and is reluctant to open up to me. Mary? Do you think he's going to like it here?"

"I'm sure he will, because he likes nature and being outdoors."

"Well, that's good. I'll show him everything around here, and of course we can go fishing too. If he likes, and I'm sure he will, we can invite Grandpa too. I'm sure he can teach us all how to catch a fish. You know, Mary, I've been thinking about buying a house in Palm Desert. The boy needs a neighborhood and some friends so they can play after school. Maybe even join a sports team, or play tennis. To live here on the ranch would be too lonesome for him. There are no neighbors and no kids."

"You know, you don't have to do that. You already have a house that would be perfectly fine for us."

"I know, but I have the money and I want to do that so our son can grow up in a normal environment. Besides, it's a good investment. We can go house hunting after I introduce you to Vic. I just called to let him know we're coming. He's my best friend and I told him all about you. So let's go to Victor's place, and then to Palm Desert. I have a friend that who a realtor. He said he would help us find the right house for us."

As they were driving, Mary mentioned how peaceful it was around there. "That's why my mother wanted to move out here," Hank said. "She enjoyed living here so much. I still miss her."

At Vic's house Hank introduced Mary, and Vic was pleased to meet her. He told her how much Hank told him about her, and that he was a lucky man.

Vic welcomed her and congratulated her and gave her a hug. She thanked him and told him how sorry she was that he lost his wife. Then Vic, with tears in his eyes, told Mary about his life.

"Rachel and I were childhood sweethearts, dating throughout high school, and then, of course, we got married. Her parents owned a stationery store in downtown San Diego, and Rachel worked at that store for some time. As for me—I worked for a software company that created bookkeeping and financial software for business. We bought a house in a suburb called La Mesa. It was nice living there, but the stress of commuting took a toll on both of us. Rachel floated the idea of moving to the country—but where? So on weekends, we took drives throughout the surrounding areas, and to make a long story short, we wound up here. We enjoyed the solitude and the idea of not jumping in the car in the morning, rain or shine, and fighting traffic to get to the job. When we came out in the morning to have coffee on the patio, Rachel would always say how fortunate we were to be able to live in this small piece of heaven. I miss her so much."

Mary said, "Hank told me the details of the accident, so you don't need to torture yourself telling me about it." With watering eyes, they hugged, and then she said to Hank, "I'm ready, if you are," as she looked at Hank.

"Okay," said Hank, "See you later, Vic," and off they went to Palm Desert.

In his friend's office they discussed the type of house, and neighborhood they were looking for. They looked at several houses before they took a break and went to lunch on El Paseo, one of the finest shopping areas in the nation. Only top quality stores and restaurants grace the boulevard. The beauty of the landscaping in the median and the art displays are really top-notch. Mary was very impressed. She compared the street to Rodeo Drive in Beverly Hills.

After lunch, they went on the prowl again to find a house. They looked at several more before seeing a very impressive house on Goldenrod, a nice street. You could see in their faces that they both seem to be pleased. So Hank said, "I think that's it." Mary nodded and Hank made an offer. Their discussions on the way home were all about the house, guesthouse, pool, and neighborhood.

The next morning, Mary got ready to go back to Ventura, and Hank had to take care of business. As she drove out the driveway, she yelled, "Say hello to Vic for me, and I love you." As she drove through Pasadena, she got a call from Hank telling her that the people selling the house accepted their offer, and in three weeks or so they could move.

"Of course, we have to do some painting and so forth and will need some furniture, but I think we can do all that after we get married."

Over the next few days and weeks, Hank made several visits to Ventura, and Mary made several trips to the ranch. One of these weekends Mary told Hank the terrible detail of treatment she got from Felix. He acted like being possessed by a demon of hate. The parents of Felix are wonderful and helped me to get away from this situation. His dad who ran the law firm had our divorce arranged and send Felix on business to Mexico City. In the meantime Mr. and Mrs. Mateo drove us, Hank junior and myself to the airport and gave me the tickets in an envelope with ten thousand Dollars and the divorce papers asking to stay in touch so they can come and visit us. In the meantime they arranged some medical help for Felix when he gets back. The departure was such a sad relieve for the four of us. The Mateo's loved Hank very much, but they realized that the condition we lived in was unhealthy for all of us. They promised to come to see us as soon as the condition presents itself.

Friday night before the wedding, Vic and Hank traveled to Studio City and took a room at the Holiday Inn. They reserved three more for Mary, Hank Jr., Mary's parents, and Mary's two best friends from college. Nancy lived in San Francisco, where she owned a small bookstore, and Andrea came down from San Jose, where she taught history in high school. The third friend from their college days, by the name of Pat Wilson did not respond to Mary's wedding invitation. The woman in their conversation discussed the memory of Pat and the last contact they had with her. Turned out that Pat Wilson became a showgirl and dancer. Nancy saw her last in her store before she moved to Las Vegas with her son. And of course, Jack lived there in town, in an area called Brentwood. He was to join them the next day at the church with his fiancée, Amelia.

At 10:00 a.m., they assembled at the church. Hank introduced everyone to the minister: "This is my mother-in-law, Maria Hamilton, this is my father-in-law, Walter Hamilton, and these young ladies are Amelia, my brother's fiancée, and Nancy and Andrea, friends of the bride. These three are the bridesmaids, and this is my son Hank, my brother Jack, and my friend Vic. These three are going to be my best men. And the bride that Mr. and Mrs. Hamilton are going to walk down the aisle is Mary—my bride, my love, my happiness."

"Very well then." The minister nodded to the organist, who started the music. Mary chose the song "You are the wind beneath my Wings." The ceremony was simple but very emotional.

After church, they went to the Ivy in Beverly Hills where they enjoyed both lunch and each other's company. Some had not seen each other for quite a while, and most were also getting to know new acquaintances. Jack invited everyone to his house for dinner and drinks. The out-of-towners all drove to their hotel, changed, and got ready to go to Jack's house.

Everyone was impressed with the neighborhood and the house. Jack had a bartender, a chef, and four helpers. At the dinner table they got to know each other better, and had a lovely time. The party broke up after midnight, and everybody said their good-byes.

Vic noticed the houses and the beautiful trees, some of them eighty feet tall. He asked, "Isn't this close to where O. J. Simpson used to live?"

"His house was around the block," said Amelia.

"I thought so," responded Vic. "It's a gorgeous neighborhood."

Because of the amount of adult beverages that had been consumed, and the need for guests to drive afterward, the host ordered a stretch limousine that waited in the driveway. On the way to the hotel, Vic seemed to be infatuated with Nancy. The two decided to visit Universal Studios and invited Hank Jr. to join them. Mr. and Mrs. Hamilton had decided to sleep in. They needed a day to rest up after all the excitement. Hank and Mary were going to take Andrea to Burbank Airport at 11:00 a.m. for her flight home to San Jose. And then it was on to Las Vegas for their honeymoon. They were to be back at the ranch on Thursday.

Sunday turned out to be a nice day for Hank Jr., and led to a passionate love affair between Nancy and Vic. The two just hit it off the first time they saw each other, and as he took her to Burbank Airport, he promised her that he would come and visit her in San Francisco the next week. Driving home on the 210 freeway, Nancy called Vic to tell him that she really enjoyed his company and had fun the day before. So Vic whistled and sang all the rest of the way home.

On Thursday, when Mary and Hank came home, Vic excitedly told them that he had fallen in love with Nancy, and that she seemed to be interested, too.

"Good for you," said Mary. "She's a nice woman, very serious, but still fun to be with. She was my roommate in college. We had some good times together. And she was always there for me and her friend from two doors down the hall. Her name was Pat Wilson and she had a crush on Hank,. I remember it well. She would say sometimes that she is going to marry Hank and have three beautiful children. Somehow we lost touch with Pat, but Nancy, Andrea and myself stuck together. When I needed a shoulder to cry on or some help with my studies Nancy was there to help anyway she could. She's brilliant and well-read; that's why she has the bookstore. I don't think there's much money in it, but she enjoys it so much that she doesn't mind the financial short comings."

The next day, Mary had to go back to Ventura, and she needed a car. So Hank took her to Palm Desert to buy a car and look at their new house. They bought a Ford Explorer, and after the tour through the house, she had to leave in order to get through the traffic before rush hour in Los Angeles and surrounding areas.

Hank and Vic had to take care of some business and some more tests. Everything seemed to be going pretty well, except they had no connection for the drugs. They began scheming again, and Hank thought the only way this was going to work would be for Vic to get the contact.

"Now, how do you propose to do that?" Vic asked.

"It's very simple. You hang around Mexicali for a day or two, don't shave or bathe for a couple days, act a little bit stoned, and they'll come to you."

"Why me," said Vic?

"Because I can't be associated with this. They see me all the time, and this conspicuous truck would put the whole operation in jeopardy."

"I see what you mean. I have no experience in this sort of thing."

"Don't worry, it's not that hard. You don't even have to do anything; just be there and look grubby, that's all."

"I hope I can pull that off."

"I think you should go with me tomorrow when I deliver to Carlos. I could drop you off at a street corner and see what happens. In the worst-case we have to try Gordo again. Of course, he's not to know that we're together or that I'm involved.

"So if you have something to say, call me from a hiding place. Don't let them see you have a phone. Whenever you're ready, call me. Stand on the same corner where I left you, and act like a hitchhiker.

"I got a call from Miranda telling me that the papers are ready for the orchard. We are now the proud owners of ten acres of Mexico for ninety-nine years."

"Why ninety-nine years?" Vic wondered.

"That's all they give you when as a foreigner. I guess we won't live that long anyway."

The next morning, off they went with a full load of poultry. Everything went smoothly at the border. Hank dropped Vic off as planned, and then went to the butcher shop and made his deliveries. Before he drove to the orchard, he saw Vic at the corner making a deal. Hank was amazed at how quickly that worked. He drove by, not looking obviously at the deal, and kept on driving out of town to pick up the papers and say good-bye to Miranda and Maria.

When Hank arrived at the farm, they had packed everything already on a pickup that Miranda rented in Pasadena. She told Hank that she got her old apartment back, and her mother really likes it there.

Miranda said, "Across the street from our apartment lives a young Mexican family with a little girl and the wife's mother. The little girl's grandmother and my mom already spoke the other day for about an hour. I'm so glad that my mom is adjusting and liking the city life."

"That's good for her and for you, and I'm sure for the lady across the street too," Hank said.

After Miranda gave Hank the papers, she started to cry and said to Hank that they could not take the dogs with them. Can you find it in your heart to let them live on the property. They are good watchdogs and warn you when strangers approach. Out here you need this type of security. They really scare me, "said Hank."

"They're supposed to scare strangers. When you live in an isolated place like this, you need to know if somebody is in the vicinity or tries to sneak up on you, because here you can scream for help all you want, but no one will hear you."

"You must come with me, so the dogs can see you and that you mean no harm, and they won't forget you. By nature, they're very loving animals."

They went into the stable where the dogs were penned up. Hank seemed nervous, and the dogs were nervous, but because of Miranda, and giving them some treats, they sniffed Hank up and down and wagged their tails. "Not too bad," he said. "They might be an asset to us. Yes, I'll take care of the dogs. I am so grateful said Miranda.

Where is your mother?"

"She's been in the orchard for hours. We have to call her because I need to get going in order to avoid some of the heavy traffic at rush hour."

"I'll get her," said Hank. When Maria saw him she also started to cry, and then she hugged him and walked briskly to the truck got in and never looked back.

Miranda came running toward him and hugged him and said, "Any time you're close to Pasadena, come and see us. I'll call you as soon as we get settled in. I'm so grateful to you. Good-bye Hank."

"Good-bye Miranda", replied Hank, and they left.

Hank drove back into town, trying to pick up Vic the hitchhiker. Sure enough, as he came to the corner, Vic was thumbing to hitch a ride. Hank picked him up, and they drove back to the orchard. On the way there, they decided that from then on they would call the ranch Miranda.

As they were driving, Vic told Hank about their connection. "He said they could supply all the coke we would ever need or want. Prices are competitive. I asked about amounts, and he said as much as we need. In the meantime, he gave me twenty ounces."

Arriving at Miranda, Hank said, "All right, let's get to it and load those birds up. Twenty ounces is no big deal. The birds were loaded in twenty minutes Hank had put the cages with the birds in the outbuilding in the back."

Vic said, "Before we let them go, they need to drink some water. They've been in these cages a long time."

"Okay," said Hank. "What do you think about the ranch?"

It was the first time Vic had a chance to see the ranch. He was impressed. He said, "Those trees look better than mine. That's a nice ten-acre orchard, I must say. And like you said, Hank, the outbuildings are all okay. Can you imagine how much you would have to pay for something like this at home?"

"Yeah, I can!"

Vic asked again about the ninety-nine-year deal.

38

"We never really own it; it's more like renting, but who cares? Ninety-nine years is a long time."

They gave the birds some water and then took them out one at a time to load them up and put them back. When they were all done, they took them in the yard and let them go. After that, they put out some more food for the dogs and headed for home.

Vic said, "You never told me about the dogs."

"What was I supposed to do? Miranda couldn't take them with her, so she asked me to please take care of them. What could I say? It was a sad good-bye and I couldn't refuse. Maybe we should put a chain-link fence around the orchard and let them watch the place. I don't think anybody would take the chance of climbing the fence with those dogs around."

"Hank, I think you're right. That would secure the property, and we could bring in some poultry and raise them here. It has all kinds of possibilities. For now, let's just see if our birds came in."

On the way home, they talked about the ladies in their lives and how happy they were. When they got home, all the birds where in their coops, including number eighteen, the one that was missing for three weeks. She still had all the weights on her.

Hank said, "We need to check her out, every bit of her. We just don't know what technology they use nowadays, either the Border Patrol or the drug cartel. Maybe she fell behind and settled with another flock, but this time she saw her own flock and followed them. We just don't know. The best thing to be safe is to take number eighteen to Los Angeles, kill her, and leave the carcass in a park, just in case there is a tracer in or on her."

It was a pleasure for them to remove all the packets, knowing that their idea worked.

"The next big challenge will be the geese; they should be hatching any day now," said Hank.

"Yeah, Hank, you can start your training program. It'll be a hoot to watch it. We'll find out who is the smartest, you or the geese."

"Oh shut up. Just think— instead of twenty ounces, the flock will bring a whole kilo. Then we'll really be in business."

Three days later, the first goslings started breaking through the shell. Within two days, they were all born and ready to train.

"We put three pigeons with ten goslings. From now on they'll spend their whole life together. We feed them together and we walk together," said Hank.

"I think that part will be a little tough, since pigeons don't like to take walks," said Vic.

"I think I'll just feed them a little at a time, popping kernels as I walk through the yard with the pigeons and goslings following me."

"This might work. If they follow the pigeons and the food at the same time, they'll get used to it."

"And when they're old enough to fly, the goslings will follow the pigeons."

Vic was laughing and said, "I got to get me a video camera; this is going to be hilarious."

"Oh shut up. You're going to look stupid if it works."

"I hope so. I could learn to look stupid. I have a good teacher." The hassle went on for quite a while, with Hank and Vic enjoying the sarcasm and wit, as always.

As the weekend approached, Vic's mind was totally consumed by his date with Nancy in San Francisco. He told Hank that he couldn't get a flight out of Palm Springs, so would be flying out of Ontario airport instead.

"That's not too bad," said Hank. "The last time I flew to the east coast I had to go to LAX, and that's a real hassle. Consider yourself lucky."

"I consider myself lucky because I'll see Nancy. I can't tell you how happy I am. This is amazing. Our happiness started because of Mary's misery."

"When is your flight?"

"At nine thirty. Nancy's going to pick me up. I hope we'll have a good time."

"I'm sure you will."

Following an uneventful flight to San Francisco, Nancy was waiting at the gate, and they hugged, kissed, and blossomed into smiles of happiness. She told him that she missed him, and he told her that he thought being apart had been the longest week of his life. She asked him what he would like to do.

"It's up to you," he replied. "I don't know this town, or anyone in it, except you."

She laughed and said, "You're under my spell, and I'll lead you astray. For starters, I made reservations on Fisherman's Wharf at a small restaurant. We'll think of something else to do until then."

The afternoon was wonderful. After lunch, they strolled through Fisherman's Wharf, then went on a short drive to Golden Gate Park, and rambled through the wonderful landscaping. They settled down on a park bench to talk about life in general. After a while she said, "Let me show you my bookstore. It's not that far from here. I want you to see it. It's my pride and joy."

"I know; Mary told me it's very nice. How is it doing financially?"

"Oh, I scrape by."

After the bookstore, they went to Nancy's apartment. It was a tiny place on the third floor, and of course, it had no elevator, so all the groceries and everything else has to be hauled up and down. *What a hassle*, Vic thought. However, he didn't say anything. She did keep everything very clean and organized.

They opened a bottle of wine, and talked about the wedding and the good times they had together a week before. Their desire for sex grew as the evening went on; with such passion that they missed the reservations they had for dinner. They just stayed in bed and got up the next morning at ten thirty.

Vic said, "I've never slept that long in my life."

Nancy said, "It's a long time for me too, sleeping in that late. However, I must say, it was wonderful, and I think I'm falling in love with you."

"It makes me so happy to hear you say that, because I fell for you from the first moment I saw you last week," said Vic. "I was very anxious all week and so nervous, not knowing what to expect. I would've been devastated if this turned out to be just a weekend fling on your part. I'm very happy the way it's turned out. It's too bad my flight back is for four in the afternoon. I know it's a short visit, but it's been wonderful. To make things a little easier, I bought a round-trip ticket for you for next Friday at 7:00 p.m., with a return flight at eight o'clock Sunday night.

She replied, "Thank you so much, I'm looking forward to it."

"Now I have to shower and clean up and get ready for my flight. Hank and I have some business to attend to in the morning, and you have to be in your bookstore. That's life's obligations interfering with our pleasure. Why don't we shower together, since I won't see you for a whole week?" said Vic.

"Good idea," said Nancy. The splashing went on until the water got cold. Talk about the need for a cold shower!

On the drive to the airport, Nancy said, "It'll be a long week. I love you and I'll miss you." They said their good-byes at the airport with tears running down her cheeks.

Vic arrived at Hank's house about 7:30 p.m. He couldn't wait to tell Hank what a wonderful weekend he had and that he and Nancy were in love. What bothered him was that he loved her so much that he would feel guilty taking her away from the bookshop.

Hank said, "Hold on—not a problem! We move the bookshop to El Paseo—better neighborhood, better clientele, nicer weather, and living with you. I'm sure that would please Nancy."

"Hank, you're a genius! It'll show when you walk the goslings. No one else could do that."

"How nice is that? I give you a solution, and you give me crap. Isn't that what you're here for?"

"Yeah, if we had to depend on you, we would still be carving stone tablets to keep records."

"Very funny said Vic," Hank then told Vic that "Mary is coming down on Thursday. She's bringing samples of different things for the house, and she can stay till Sunday night."

"That's great. Then Mary can drop Nancy off at the airport."

"I guess so," said Hank. "I'm going to call her first thing in the morning to tell her that you and Nancy are an item, and that she's coming down on the weekend to the desert. She'll be pleased to have a friend living in the same town, especially her best friend Nancy."

In the morning, Hank found out that Nancy had called Mary, so Mary already knew all about it.

Everyone was busy that whole week. Vic was occupied with the trees, with some kind of feeding program, and with flooding the orchard. Hank was training the goslings and the pigeons. He figured out right away that he needed to trim the wings of the pigeons. That way they *had* to walk. And of course, the pigeons would follow the food. They're faster than the goslings, so the goslings wound up behind the pigeons—just as planned.

When Vic saw that, he curled up laughing. He said, "I know I should have bought that video camera. I could have made some money putting it on YouTube."

Hank said, "Yeah, with ideas like that you would starve to death."

Mary arrived on Thursday afternoon, this time with their son, and Hank Sr. was very happy to see them. They discussed all sorts of activities they could pursue, but when the boy saw all the fowl, he had no desire to do anything else except watch the birds. He visited every cage, and observed the staff loading the trucks with six hundred chickens. Mary and Hank had to take some things to their new house, but Junior refused to go with them. So Hank told Diego his foreman to take care of his son while they were gone.

Hank and Mary went to their new house. They had an appointment with the painter the following morning. Hank called him to check if he could come over to the house that afternoon. Then they wouldn't have to get up early in the morning to go there again. The painter told them that he was on a job in Redlands, and it was impossible for him to come over that day, but said, "If you can't do it tomorrow morning, let's make it on Saturday, any time you want."

Hank said, "Noon is good. I'll buy you lunch, and thanks for changing our appointment."

Hank and Mary looked through the house and discussed things like colors and furniture. They kissed in every room and wound up naked in the pool. Hank said, "The house already feels like home." Mary agreed.

They picked up some pizza on the way home and called Vic to join them. They had a nice evening, and of course, Vic told them how happy he was, and how much he loves Nancy—as if

Mary didn't already know that, but she didn't want to dampen his enthusiasm.

Vic also told her about Hank's idea to move the bookshop to Palm Desert, and that he hoped she would like the idea. "I'm willing to buy a house in Palm Desert so we could live not too far from each other, and you two could enjoy each other's company."

"I don't see why not," Mary said. "I know the shop isn't doing too well, so maybe it would be better here, and she would still be with her beloved books."

The next day, Mary, Hank, and Hank Jr. went shopping in La Quinta and Palm Desert. They furnished practically the whole house. Next they needed to push the painter, who was going to stop by the next day.

Vic was all dolled up to pick up Nancy at Ontario airport. These two lovebirds didn't even come home. They rented a room in Ontario and stayed there all night.

Vic told Nancy about the plan to move the bookshop to Palm Desert. She said, "I don't know. I have to think about it. After all, I have some customers to keep me going. Yes, I really have to think about that."

In the morning, Hank called Vic and asked him where he was. Vic told them he was on his way home and asked Hank if they wanted to join them for lunch at California Pizza Kitchen. "Sounds good, we'll be there in an hour and a half, I'll see you later," Hank replied. It was a nice reunion for lunch, and Nancy was very impressed with El Paseo.

After lunch, they went to the new house. Nancy was astonished by how much room people have here for parking and recreation. "The large house, the pool—this is like a new world to me," she said. "I had no idea people live like that. I've always been buried in my books."

Mary told her she would love it so much if she would be willing to move. Vic went down on his knees and proposed marriage as Nancy burst out in tears. With a tiny, squeaky voice she said, "I will."

Vic hugged her and wiped her tears and told her how happy he was. "For good luck, we should try getting a date at the Little Brown

Church in the San Fernando Valley. Everything good came out of there." Nancy just nodded.

After Mary discussed all the colors with the painter, they went to Vic's ranch. Nancy was taken in by its peaceful environment. "Why we can't live here?" she asked.

Vic said, "That's impossible. The traffic in the morning is unbelievable on the 111 to get to the store. Besides, it gets boring around here. I think if Hank didn't live here, I would have been long gone. I can run this business from Palm Desert. I don't have to be here every day. And other people take care of the orchard.

"To live in Palm Desert would be a nice change for me too. You'll see; when we find a house and you get used to the area, you'll like it. And if you don't, we can always come back."

"Vic, I don't want to be a financial liability to you. That's the reason I'm being cautious."

"You don't have to worry about that. I make enough money for both of us, and I don't plan on taking any with me. We'll have the bookstore moved, and you can spend as much or as little time as you like, and profit is optional."

"I don't know how I deserve that, it's so wonderful. Mary, do you think you can stop by at the Little Brown Church on your way home, to check what dates are available, and book us right away?"

"Of course, I'll be happy to do that," replied Mary.

On Saturday night, they had reservations at the LG Restaurant. The group had a lovely dinner and good conversations. Even Hank Jr. thought the food was great, and Hank Sr. told all the waiters that this young man is his son. Everyone saw Hank was very proud of his boy.

Sunday morning they all slept in. At eleven, Hank invited everybody for brunch. They barbecued some hamburgers, hot dogs, and corn on the cob, and enjoyed a nice afternoon. Hank Jr., who Hank Sr. decided to start calling Henry, kept busy watching all the different fowl. And to top it off, Vic took Henry to his ranch and let two sets of pigeons fly, the highlight of the day for him.

In the meantime, the ladies got ready for their trip: Nancy to wrap up her life in San Francisco, and Mary to wait out the school year with Hank Jr. in Ventura. Before long both women were also making their weekly trips back to the Imperial Valley. These cherished visits were priceless to all five of them, but not to the grandparents.

One week at the ranch started with routine business chores and Hank's bird training program. The goslings responded really well, so they planned a training flight from Mexico for the first time. Vic and Hank decided that both of them should go on this trip. As they got ready in the morning, Vic reminded Hank that they have to take some dog food with them. Hank replied, "No, not this time. Last Thursday I took ten bags over there."

"Okay, then let's go," said Vic.

After their delivery to the butcher shop they went on to the orchard. "From now on, let's call the orchard Miranda," suggested Hank.

"Okay," said Hank. "Here is the turnoff already."

As they drove in, the dogs barked wildly, and Hank had to calm them down. Afterward, they prepped all the pigeons and took them out in the middle of the yard. Then they let them go all at the same time. As soon as the pigeons flew the first circle, the geese got excited and loud and lifted off to follow the pigeons. They made three big circles, and then they were gone.

Hank said, "I believe they're going to follow them."

Hank said, "I'm sure of it. They did at home."

Then they did some chores, namely watering, let the dogs run around to give them some exercise, secured everything, and drove home.

On the way home, they talked about their new lives and how happy they were. Arriving home and seeing all the pigeons and geese back in their cages caused both of them to feel good. To their surprise, everything was working according to their plans. So Hank, of course, had to rub it in and said, "I don't look so stupid now."

Replying, Vic said, "I'm so sorry, you're Highness, my master, my Lord."

Hank replied, "Oh, shut up. We don't know how long it took for the birds to get back home. Next time you'll stay home so we can time them. And I think they can carry quite a bit more than what we put on this time. It's such a short distance that I think they could carry a quarter pound each. That, of course, would make it worth our while. We increase the weight slowly and time them so we know exactly how much they can carry and how long it would take them to get back. We have to know every detail before we load them up with junk. Our numbering system works very well, which we can use to count how many trips each one completes, also their times, and the best and fastest leaders and followers.

In the early evening, they sat on the patio having some beers, both men rather quiet and deep in thought. Hank was scratching his head, and then revealed that he had no interest in smuggling drugs anymore.

"So what the hell are we doing this for?" Vic asked. "We've spent a lot of money and time on that project, and now you want to quit."

"I have a family now and a son to raise. You're getting married, and maybe will have some children. We shouldn't have any part in an enterprise that destroys lives."

"I agree," said Vic, "but why are we spending all this time and money on it?"

"Well, I was thinking we should perfect the airborne fleet and then sell everything, since we planned to live in Palm Desert anyway."

"How do you plan on doing that? You can't just put a sign out there and try to sell something like that."

"Of course not, but the right people would pay a lot of money for it. All we have to do is shop around for someone already in the business. It's probably going to take a while, but I think we can do it. And by that time we will have our fleet ready to fly."

Meanwhile, they hatched another five dozen goslings.

Hank said, "We have to pick twenty of them: four layers, and the rest will be in training. In two days, we can sterilize the brood house and put another sixty goose eggs into the brooder. The rest will be ducks for Carlos. He told me recently that he sells a lot of ducks and Cornish game hens. I have 240 at my place that I don't have to deliver to our stores in Los Angeles. So we're good."

The weekend arrived with great anticipation for all involved. Mary came back with the date for Nancy and Vic's wedding. Vic was picking up Nancy. When they arrived, Hank already had steaks on the barbecue, and in a few minutes they had dinner ready.

Mary looked for Hank Jr. to call him for dinner. Worried and frustrated, she came back and told Hank to go and look for him. Panic-stricken, they all spread out to look for Junior. Finally, they saw him through the trees coming toward them. He had taken his shirt off, and was carrying and cuddling a baby opossum. "He really loves animals," said Hank. "We've got to get him a dog and a cat."

"One thing at a time," said Mary. "I don't want to spoil him. With every pet there comes responsibility, and they'll take time away from his studies."

The next day the grown-ups went to Palm Desert. Nancy and Vic looked for a house for themselves. They also contacted a commercial realtor to find them a proper location for Nancy's bookstore.

Mary and Hank were busy at the house. Mary had her car loaded with dishes, glasses, silverware, and knickknacks. All had to be brought into the house and be placed in cabinets and closets. In the afternoon, Nancy and Vic came by the house all excited, because they found the house of their dreams and wanted Mary and Hank to see it. So they all jumped in the car and drove a few blocks, and there it was. The realtor showed them the property. It was very impressive, they all liked it very much, and Vic made an offer on the house.

The rest of the weekend was uneventful but pleasant. Sunday night, the women got ready and went on their routine trip to the airport, and Mary and the boy went back to Ventura. Before the boy stepped in the car, he asked his dad to be sure and take care of Buddy, his new baby opossum friend. Hank assured him that he would do his best to take care of him.

During the week, they made some more progress with their little air force. It was certainly amazing how well these bubble brain ideas came to fruition and actually worked. Hank said, "We have the capacity now to deliver at least one kilo, or around two pounds per day. It should be worth a lot of money to have that capacity without too much risk or expense. But before I start looking for a buyer, we better prepare ourselves for any and all possibilities of something backfiring on us.

"First of all, we need to launch them from different locations and at different times of the day. Also, to ensure a clean break between us and the new owners, we need to install cameras and listening devices in the outbuildings and office and also hide some around the yard, so we can get a heads up in case they try to get back at us and blame us if they get caught. We should install listening devices and cameras on the Mexican property too, and also chain-link fence. Once all that's done I'll try to find somebody from the cartels that has the financial capacity to buy your place and our air force. I think I'll start with Gordo at the Temblor. He's always up to no good, and he knows the worst kind of people. Also, I have something on him that might prevent him from talking to the law for money. I know he loves his freedom more than most, since he had a taste of the alternative lifestyle."

The following week, Hank stopped by at the Temblor to have a beer and talk to Francisco. Following the regular greetings and inquiries how everyone is, Hank floated vaguely the idea that he knows someone who has the capacity to smuggle at least five or six kilograms of cocaine every five to ten days, but he's in the hospital, and doesn't know how bad off he is, or whether he will survive.

"So the friend asked Hank if he would be interested in buying his operation," Hank continued. "But Francisco, you know how it is when you lose your freedom and you're always surrounded by scum. I was in prison only a short time, and you were in a little longer, but I think we both know that we never want to go back there. So I told him that I wasn't interested.

"Besides, I'm ready to retire. I bought a little place in the Bahamas on the beach and I want to sell everything and move there. I'm tired of this rat race. What do you think something like that would be worth to the cartel or an independent contractor?"

Francisco replied, "I don't deal in such things. I just use a little bit once in a while. That's why I had the two ounces that I sold to you. But if I hear something, I'll let you know next time you stop by."

Hank said, "No hurry. I just wanted to know to tell my friend next time I see him in the hospital so he doesn't worry so much, because his medical bills are already around eighty thousand dollars, and there's no end in sight."

"I can see your friend is in financial trouble. I'll spread the word to help your friend. See you soon, take care amigo, adios till next time."

"Good-bye, Francisco see you soon," Hank responded.

The following busy days were really a rat race. There was the installation of cameras and listening devices at Vic's place; then the counteroffer on Vic and Nancy's house came in. Hank Jr.'s school was done for the year, so Mary and the boy came to live in the new house. Also, Vic found a nice store on El Paseo that used to be a clothing store. They installed shelves and lighting to convert it into a bookstore. And Vic and Nancy booked their wedding for the following week.

The deliveries had to be made on a regular basis. Mary was overwhelmed, so she called her parents to give them a helping hand, and told them they could stay in the guesthouse as long as they wanted to. Junior was very happy about that. He loved his grandparents very much, and they also seemed to have more time for him. Hank Jr. brought his friend the opossum to the house in a brand new cage they picked up at Pet Smart. He played and took care of the opossum, and the rest of the time he spent in the pool with his grandpa watching him. The boy felt the love and nurturing in his new environment. He still bears scars from his stepdad Felix, and never asked even once regarding his whereabouts.

A tumultuous week with all this chaos and stress slowly came to a climax. It was Friday morning when Nancy, Vic, Mary, and Hank took off for Studio City. As they checked in to the Holyday Inn, Andrea walked into the lobby and greeted everyone. They all went to their rooms to change from sweat suits and T-shirts into their formal wear, then crammed into Mary's Ford Explorer, and drove off to church. Hank's brother Jack and his fiancée Amelia were already at the church. After greetings and hugs they still had ten minutes until the ceremony. The pastor came out to check if everyone in the wedding was present. So Hank said they all were there, and he introduced Nancy as the bride this time.

"Pleased to meet you," said the pastor, and then he said to Hank, "You're a windfall for my business. Seems to me just two months ago you got married to another lady."

"No, this man over there is the groom," Hank said, pointing to Vic.

"Well, another dream shattered. I already saw you coming in here four or five times a year. As a matter fact, I had big plans for the money I was going to make with you." Everyone was laughing.

Hank said, "I'm just the *best* man," with emphasis on "best," provoking another laugh.

"Now seriously, let's do this," said the pastor. He nodded to the organist, and she started playing "We've Only Just Begun." This man always delivers an emotional, romantic ceremony.

After the wedding, they went to Spagos Restaurant in Beverly Hills for a late lunch. During lunch they decided to accept Hank's invitation to spend the weekend at the ranch. He said, "We have those two houses on the property. Jack and Amelia can stay in Mom's old house and Andrea can stay in my house with us. Vic's house isn't far away, where he and Nancy, the newlyweds, will stay."

"Sounds good," everyone agreed.

"Let's go back to the hotel and collect our things," said Hank. "All right, everybody in their cars, and off we go to the Imperial Valley," where they did a nice barbecue and had a pleasant evening.

In the morning, Hank and Mary had to go to Palm Desert to check on their son and on Mary's parents, and also go shopping for groceries to feed and entertain their friends. They left a note on the kitchen table telling where they went, that they were coming back, and would be bringing lunch for everyone.

Around nine o'clock Amelia decided to check out some of those fancy stores on El Paseo in Palm Desert. Jack got up to enjoy the stillness of the desert, walking toward Hank's house and smelling the coffee. As he went in the kitchen, Andrea was sitting at the table drinking coffee.

"Good morning, Jack," said Andrea.

"Good morning, Andrea. Where is everybody?"

"Mary and Hank went shopping for groceries. They'll be back by noon. Where's Amelia?" she asked.

Hank answered that she went shopping to El Paseo and would be having lunch over there. "We're not getting along that well lately. This spat today was her not wanting to come. She's just a spoiled brat. She told me, 'I'm not a farmer and I don't like roughing it.' She probably thought that Hank was in a cabin with a potbelly stove. She was surprised to see how modern the house and everything in it is, but is huffy anyway. I don't care anymore; it's been like this for some time."

Andrea said, "Let me get you some coffee."

"That would be nice. Thank you, Andrea."

As she brought the coffee, Jack thanked her and asked if she was seeing anyone. "No, not at this time," she said, "although I was in a relationship for about a year that fizzled out very similarly to what just happened to you: first the complaints, then the bickering, and then the split."

"Well if you're interested in a relationship, I'm available," Jack said.

"You mean you're breaking up with Amelia?" As she was asking, his cell phone rang. It was Amelia breaking up with him. She told him he could pick up his car at the Palm Springs Airport. She was taking a private jet home.

"You see what I mean?" Jack said, and laughed. "She's a spoiled brat."

"Another cup?" Andrea asked.

"Yeah, why not?" and as she came back with the coffee pot, he got up and kissed her as he tried to hug her.

He touched the coffee pot. "Ouch!" he said, "That's hot."

She replied, "That's not the only thing hot." She put the pot down and they started making out. Needless to say, they wound up in bed and had a wonderful time.

After things calmed down a bit, Andrea said, "It looks like we both had a long hiatus."

"Yes, you're right. It hasn't been good with Amelia and me for some time—as a matter of fact, for a long time. I'm so glad I decided to come here this weekend."

"So am I," she replied.

"This was so spontaneous. If it was just a spur of the moment sexual encounter and nothing more, I understand, because we're both very vulnerable," said Jack.

"I thank you, Jack, I needed it," said Amelia.

". As a matter of fact, when I found out that you were going to the desert, I insisted on going, and that started this latest fight we had. It was sort of an unplanned plan that somehow took its course in the right direction. I'm grateful for that."

"Well, I tell you Jack, I'm falling in love with you."

Jack said, "After this gloomy beginning, it's turning into the best weekend ever. We have to make plans. For now, let's just get cleaned up before the others arrive, and we can tell them what happened. Are they going to be surprised, or what?"

"Pleasantly I hope," said Andrea.

"I'm sure Hank is going to be happy about it. He's never liked Amelia. He's always said that she's spoiled and stuck up. That's the reason we never saw much of each other the last couple of years. Mary, Nancy, and Vic, haven't known her, so it probably makes no difference to them.

"Well, don't worry about anything. I'm going to Mom's house to shower and change. Gosh, just saying 'Mom's house' sounds so pleasant and comforting. I still miss her when she appears in my thoughts. I'll see you in about twenty minutes. I should be done by then."

By the time Andrea came out of the shower, Mary and Hank were unloading the groceries. Mary said, "Good afternoon, sleepyhead."

"I guess I have that coming," Andrea replied. "Can I help you with the groceries?"

"Sure, there are some more in the car."

"I'll bring them in. Where is your husband?"

"Hank went over to wake Amelia and Jack."

Andrea began, "Let me tell you something Mary. They're not sleeping anymore. Amelia left this morning to go shopping in El Paseo. Jack came over and we had coffee together. I thought it was kind of odd that she would prefer shopping to sleeping in. Turns out the two had a fight, one of many, and he told me that she's very spoiled. Hank told me that too, but he didn't predict a breakup. When Jack told me that, they had not broken up yet, but when I served him a second cup of coffee, he stood up and kissed me."

"You're kidding? Then what happened," Mary asked.

"Well, to make a long story short, one thing led to another and we wound up in bed."

"Why, you little slut!"

"It wasn't only my idea. We both were in desperate need. His fiancée called just a little earlier and told him he could pick up his car at the Palm Springs Airport. That news made it very easy for me to give him what he wanted, and I think I wanted it even more."

"I'm stunned," Mary said. "But I'm so happy for you. This is wonderful."

At that moment, Hank opened the door with a big grin on his face and said, "Congratulations to both of you, Andrea. Jack will be here in a few minutes, and as soon as Vic and Nancy arrive, we'll toast with champagne." Then he walked over to Andrea and hugged her.

At that point, Nancy, Vic, and Jack came through the door. Everybody was smiling, they all knew what had happened, and congratulated Jack and Andrea. Hank proposed a toast to the new couple, then to their friendship, and then to health and happiness. They had a wonderful lunch, as a matter of fact, a wonderful day and evening, and the new couple spent the night together.

Sunday morning Hank had to drive Jack to Palm Springs to fetch his car. They came back just in time for lunch. The ladies had all that time to themselves and took full advantage of it. All morning, they felt like teenagers, giggling and just enjoying life. After lunch, Jack and Andrea had to leave to avoid some of the heavy Sunday night traffic in Los Angeles. Jack dropped her off at Burbank airport. They wouldn't see each other all week, but the next weekend, Jack was flying to San Jose, so they could have that weekend together.

In the meantime, at the ranch, Mary and Nancy went to Palm Desert to do some shopping and then went to see Mary's family. Afterward, they went to see the completed bookstore. The new shelving and lighting were awesome. The books and Nancy's personal belongings were scheduled for delivery on Thursday. They also stopped by at Vic and Nancy's new house. Escrow would be closing in the middle of the following week, and then everyone was going to be busy.

Hank and Vic were taking care of their chores, and of course the delivery and all the rest. On his previous trip, Hank stopped by the cantina to have a beer and talk again to Francisco. As he entered the cantina, he noticed that it was the first time the cantina had so many people in it, especially on a weekday and in the middle of the morning.

"Hello, Hank," said the barkeep.

"Hi, Francisco, looks like business is picking up. What's with all these people here? Is it a special holiday or a meeting of some fraternity?"

Francisco responded, "Sort of," he said. "I put the word out about your friend's dilemma. These are interested parties. The demand for safe transport is very high. To get drugs across the border is almost impossible at this point. Digging a tunnel is risky, because some of them get discovered before you get to use them. In addition, the money you spent on labor and materials is lost. If you're talking about an immediate solution for delivering their goods, that would fetch up to a million dollars."

"Well my friend, the operation for sale is a lot bigger than that. I think, Francisco, you're talking to beginners. The operation my friend has is around six million plus."

"Oh, amigo, I don't know if somebody can come up with that much cash. Like I said, you're not talking to the pros."

"If they find out how well it works, it might bring even more. From what he told me, once you have the knowledge you can double it or triple it as many times as you like."

It is a system that works from many locations"

"It could be the bread and butter for some cartel. They usually have more money than they can spend. Francisco responded by saying that he will find someone to buy your friends operation. I have to go to Acapulco tomorrow. I can talk to some people down there that run the bigger operations. Okay I'll see you next week when you get back ", Francisco."

"Wait a minute, step into my office. I want to talk to you before you leave." He waved to one guy and said something in Spanish. Hank and Francisco went into the back room that the fat man called his office. This was a huge room with all the comforts you can think of.

Hank looked around and said, "You son of a bitch—you're in the cartel!"

Francisco answered yes.

"So why do you lie to me?"

"One can't be too careful."

"All right, let's cut the crap and get down to business. The price is ten million, take it or leave it. The property involved has to be bought legally by a person or a company, with checks going through title search and escrow. The cost of those properties is on top of the ten million cash. All I want to hear from you is yes or no."

"Why so harsh?" asked Francisco.

"Because you lied to me."

"Hank you're lying to me too, and still are. It's your operation is it not?"

"Yes, it is. So what do you say?"

"I say yes, but to get you the money will take several weeks, because we don't take money back to the States. We'll accumulate it in California."

"All right. The details I have to work out with my people. As soon as we have the money, I'll train two people only, and leave after the second successful delivery. The deal and everything else will be documented—photographed, and described in every detail. I'll have two people holding exact copies of the details, one on the East Coast and one on a farm in the Midwest. They're both very good friends of mine. In case of a double-cross, they'll send copies to the proper authorities and district attorneys. And two copies will be sent to the competition, meaning other cartels. And for backup insurance I programmed my computer to send email to all law enforcement agencies in this States and Mexico in case you plan something stupid. In case I don't show up at my computer, within 24 hours, you're toast. If you're still in, we will shake hands. If not, tell your troops to stay away from me, or you will never see the morning sun again."

"Amigo, you know I'm your friend."

"I hope so," said Hank. "I know where you've been, and the people you were forced to associate with, the scum of the earth. You were in their quite a while and learned a lot from them. Don't use any of this crap on me. I know you have your soldiers in the bar right now. If something happens to me, I'll still watch you take your last breath, and that goes for all of you in this cantina. My safety is your responsibility. Now let's have a beer."

Francisco grabbed the phone and said, *"Abilio dos cervesas."* A man with a lot of tattoos and a shaved head entered the room with two bottles of beers in hand.

Hank acted clumsy and dropped the bottle on the floor, saying, "I'm so sorry, just give me a glass from the tab. That Corona will do." Hank, of course, dropped the bottle on purpose, not trusting Francisco anymore. They drank the beers, and then Hank left through the back door.

Hank took a lot of pictures with his cell phone to start documenting people and places. Then he went back through the same door and told Francisco, to find somebody a legitimate name or company to put the properties in for escrow. "I'll see you on Thursday. I hope you'll have all your ducks in a row."

"This comment from a poultry man is very funny and special," said Francisco.

"Cut the crap," said Hank, and drove off.

As soon as Hank was across the border, he phoned Vic to ask him where he was, who replied he was on his way to Palm Desert.

"Where are you physically?"

He answered, "I'm on highway 111, driving through La Quinta, on my way to Palm Desert." Hank said, "Turn around Vic. I need to talk to you."

"What's the matter? Are you okay?" asked Vic.

"I'm fine; I'll see you at your place in fifteen minutes."

"All right, see you."

They arrived at Vic's place at the same time. Vic asked right away what the problem was. Hank looked around and said, "No problem." The tension at this point was so extreme, that the men looked pale. "Let's go inside your office."

"All right," said Vic."You're acting very strange."

Hank finally said, "I sold your place and the Mexican orchard. For how much? Well, we have to call an appraiser to see how much it's worth. And the Mexican orchards we will sell for fifty thousand."

"But that's wonderful, since we already bought the homes in Palm Desert. Hank, you're a wheeler-dealer. I must say—you did very well."

"I know it's a good deal, but I sold our airborne fleet for ..."

But Vic interrupted and said, "You really did well, and I knew this other idea is a joke."

"No, not really," said Hank. "It worked well, and it's worth money. Even more than you would've gotten for the video that you never made."

Vic replied, "If you're so hung up on it, once we get the money from the ranch, I'll give you some money for your troubles and for your expenses on the so-called air force."

"Shut up. Vic—I did sell it."

"How much, did you at least get some of your expenses covered?"

"Yes I did," said Hank. "I sold that stupid idea for a lot of money."

"You're kidding. Let me guess: twenty, thirty grand? A little more—forty, fifty? We paid more than that for the truck."

"I know, so I sold it for ten million dollars."

"Are you nuts?"

"Maybe I am, but I did sell it for ten million dollars."

There was a long pause; then Vic said, "You're not kidding, are you?"

"No, that *is* what I sold it for. I just seem to have a knack for stupid ideas."

"All right Hank, you made your point."

"What I'm trying to say is next time you think I'm doing something stupid, wait at least until it fails before you start laughing."

"Point well taken," answered Vic.

"I'll call an appraiser in the morning and see what the value is for the orchard. Last time I heard, it was twenty-five thousand per acre. That would bring it up to three and a half million bucks. I sure hope it all works out. If it does, we're set."

The land appraisal came in at $28,400 per acre. That made its value $3,976,000 plus the house and outbuildings. The total came in at $4,312,000.

Vic said, "This turned out to be a good investment. Rachel and I paid $1,212,000 for this property and made a good living with the orchard. And you and I had some pretty good times."

Hank said, "Now I know how Miranda and her mother felt when they had to leave their place to start a new life in Pasadena. The similarities are uncanny. We're starting our new lives in Palm Desert. Go figure."

Hank had to deliver the poultry to Carlos and then work on the deal with Gordo. He went to see Francisco to get more information from him and a name for the ownership of the orchard. Hank told him the purchaser had to be an American citizen with the resources to buy the place. Francisco told Hank, "The information you need is all in this envelope, with instructions from a law firm in Chicago. Names, addresses, e-mail, and phone numbers are all there."

"That's good," said Hank. "Thank you."

"You want a beer?" Gordo asked.

Hank answered, "No, I've got too much to do today. I'll see you in a few days."

"Okay, amigo. Adios."

Hank said good-bye and drove to the orchard.

He fed the dogs and let the birds go. As he was driving out to the street, he turned around and decided to take the dogs with him, since he promised Miranda that he would take care of them. His conscience kicks in every once in a while. For some reason, this character is very compassionate and loving when it comes to people or animals he has to care for. He put the dogs in plain sight in the poultry cages Since he came through the border three or four times a week, no one bothered to check out the cargo. The idea of a very conspicuous truck that came from Vic, paid off again. The hassle with the dogs, not having papers or immunizations could have caused a lot of problems. Hank is a problem solver and problem creator. If he has no one to love or care for, he always turns to drugs, alcohol, or just bad behavior. It happened in college when he had no care in the world. He was really good and loving when his mother was alive and they were living together. After his mother passed away, he had another relapse, and now with this new life, he has his wife, Mary, his son, Hank Jr., and his friend Vic, and is growing closer to his brother, Jack. In that kind of setting Hank becomes very loving and caring. He's very loyal person, sharp, and a quick thinker outside the box. But sometimes he sounds like the most brutal Mafia boss.

While Hank was gone, the books arrived at the bookshop. Nancy was busy directing the placement of books and memorabilia at the store. She beamed with a reserved smile, as if she were meeting a longing lover, when she saw her books. The satisfaction and joy was written all over her. Nancy loves her books.

Vic went to the escrow office to take possession of their new house. With the key in hand, he did a walk-through with the realtor, made a few phone calls to arrange for a cleaning crew, and then he called the painter who painted Hank and Mary's house. Also, the pool man left his card, so Vic called him too and introduced himself as the new owner, saying that that he would like to keep him on. While he was still on the phone, the gardener showed up, so Vic went out and talked to him, and kept him on as their gardener. *A lot accomplished within a short time*, he thought to himself.

Then he went to see Nancy at the bookstore. Things were going pretty well, and he was amazed how the store looked with the books in it. In the evening, they had a chance to check the lights and adjust and point them at art and other focal points.

Mary was assimilating into the new environment with their son, with some big help from her parents. They informed Mary that they had to go back to Ventura to take care of some personal matters and their house. Of course, she knew that day was coming. It was even harder for Junior. He cried when they announced that they had to go.

So his grandpa asked him if he would like to go fishing to Lake Cachuma with him. Of course, he jumped at the chance. He always had a good time with Grandpa, especially on their fishing trips. The following days, Mary helped Nancy to arrange things for the house, and furnish it.

The men were busy getting things lined up for the takeover by the new owners. That lawyer from Chicago sent over two guys to enter into a training program. Hank picked them up from Los Angeles International Airport at 11:30 p.m. in a closed van. Meanwhile, Vic took all phones, files, and computers out of his place. Then he activated the listening devices and cameras they recently installed. Hank told those two that they were not allowed to have a phone or cameras until the deal went through. Both handed over their phones, and Hank thanked them, saying, "Business is business."

When the three arrived at the ranch, Vic made sure they saw the Dobermans when he showed them their sleeping quarters. Hank went to his farm to watch the trainees on his computer screen. As soon as things settled down, they pulled out a cell phone. Hank immediately turned the microphone on and said in a disguised voice, "If my boss finds out you tried to call, he will kill you. Take the phone and put it in the sink and fill it with water. Then hide it, so if they find it you can say it doesn't work. Did they fail to tell you that you're under total surveillance?" They both answered no. Hank told them, "One of my bosses likes it when he has an excuse to torture somebody. I think he gets pleasure from hurting people."

Hank went to see Francisco in the morning and asked the pre determent afternoon delivery of the cash in a remote area of Death

Valley near Scotty's Castle. That was discussed and agreed upon. After the fat man told him, that they don't have it quite together at this point. "Obviously a stall tactic." And Hank got a little perturbed to put it mildly, as he was raising his voice and pointing with his finger in to the fat man's face.

"If you don't have the money by tomorrow morning, you'll leave me no choice. I'll have to kill the two guys that you sent from Chicago, and the deal is off. And if you try to make a big deal out of it, or try to rescue them, you'll go to heaven too. If you think this is a game, it's the last game you'll play."

Then Gordo said, "Amigo, why so hostile?"

Hank replied, "I put my ass on the line training your people, and now that they know how to operate my system, you want to skip paying for it. You think you can outmaneuver me. Lucky for you that you weren't successful. Your life expectancy would have been cancelled; your life would have been shorter than a bad commercial on television. From now on, you'll have to deal with the cartel."

"No," said Francisco. "This is just a misunderstanding. I think that the guys brought the money to San Diego."

"Listen, Gordo: I'll give you one more chance. Tomorrow morning, at four o'clock in the morning, at Caesar's Palace in Las Vegas, I want a driver alone in a van parked at the rear parking structure right next to the elevator on the third level with the money in it. The van next to that parking space will be unlocked. Inside will be a sign in the back saying 'Deposit here.' That car will have a remotely activated bomb in it. If this person doesn't exactly follow instructions, both vehicles will get eliminated. Evidence regarding you and your cartel will be in the mail the minute the instruction are ignored. "The money has to be packed in cardboard boxes that are clearly marked 'shampoo.' Print up believable-looking labels, just in case someone sees them. Also one carton must have shampoo in it, marked 1 of 20 in the event that security wants to see what these cartons contain. That box needs to be in the back, just in case. While your driver is transferring the money into the van next to him with the back gate open, the driver of our van will transfer the remote-controlled bomb into your vehicle and leave a cell phone on the front seat. The bomb is going to be in a man's shoulder bag. After he loads the money, the driver of your car needs to drive toward Hoover Dam and wait till he gets a phone call on the cell phone that was left on the seat on the passenger side. He's not to touch the phone until it rings. Then he should answer it and follow instructions. Make sure he doesn't carry a cell phone or a watch or anything metal that could set the wrong things in motion.

"You know the amounts. Just so there is no misunderstanding, I'll tell you only one more time, so pay attention. Your life depends on it.

"We need a cashier's check for $1,500,000 made out to Imperial Valley Citrus to put into escrow that will show 'paid in full.' The actual value per appraisal is $28,400 per acre times 140 acres, which comes to $3,976,000, plus the buildings. That brings it to $4,385,000. In addition to the cashier's check you need $2,885,000 in cash; you need $50,000 in cash for the orchard in Mexico, plus the ten million for the rest. So the total cash due is $12,935,000. If you agree, say yes. Otherwise, the two guys that you sent from Chicago are going to buy the farm figuratively. They just know too much already."

"You're so brutal. I thought you were my friend."

"I was until I found out that you want to cheat me out of everything. Just to be sure that you understand what I told you, to prove that I know how you think, and that I'll always be ahead of you, here is a DVD with the information on it that I just told you. And that anticipation about the money not being ready should scare the hell out of you.

"I also know how high you rank in this cartel, and that they helped you to escape from prison. I can't trust you anymore. That's why I need insurance, and right now the only insurance I can accept is the money."

"Yes, I agree, amigo. "Said Francisco

"Okay then, and don't ever try any bullshit on me again. This is the only pardon you will ever get from me." I am not the Governor.

"I'm sorry Hank, this won't happen again. It wasn't my idea. You know how these organizations work. I want to be your friend."

"That respect you have to earn, so make sure that everything goes smoothly tomorrow. I know it sounds like a lot of money, but you guys make that in a few days. Plus you're getting rid of some competition, namely my organization. See you next time, hopefully alive, not in a casket."

As soon as Hank was across the border, he phoned Vic to tell him to pack a few things for an overnight trip to Las Vegas. Call the women to let them know; tell them we have to go to Los Angeles so they don't worry. When Hank arrived at Vic's place, Hank informed him about the deal that he made, and how they should proceed. "First we drive to La Quinta and rent a Suburban that we drive to Las Vegas where we'll also rent a van. Then I'll drive the van to Caesar's Palace to the rear parking structure and park it in the second space from the elevator on the right side on the third level. We have to do that before four in the morning. I don't think that in the middle of the week we will have a problem parking there. We also have to stop to buy a cell phone and activate it. There are some available without a contract that requires you to buy a certain amount of minutes. We have to make a sign, so we need some paper, a Sharpie, a box, and some packing tape to make it look like a bomb. We'll just put a bunch of batteries in it and pack it tight so it doesn't rattle. We also need a cheap shoulder bag to put the box inside of."

"What is the bag for?" Vic asked.

"I'll tell you later." Hank couldn't tell Vic about the details, because the stress would have incapacitated him. "We take a room at the MGM. They have RV parking in the back where we can transfer the money. Then you take the van back to Hertz, come back in a cab, go through the Casino, and come out the back. As soon as we're out of town I'll call the delivery guy to start the car and drive to Hoover Dam, handling the shoulder bag very gently, and will throw it and the cell phone off the dam from the high side to make it look like it was accidental, while trying to take a picture with the phone, because I'm sure that the dam is under constant surveillance.

Vic said, "Oh my God, you never told me that it had to have a camera; the store is closed by now."

"Chill out, the guy isn't really going to take pictures. And he'll be glad to get rid of the bomb."

"I always wonder where you dig up all that bullshit."

Hank said, "That little stint in the slammer was the best and fastest education I ever experienced."

The slow start in the morning seemed like a sleepy affair. Hank and Vic drove to Caesar's Palace, not saying very much. As they came closer to their destination, stress was noticeable on their faces, especially on Vic's. They entered the sparsely occupied parking structure and drove slowly to the third level to the designated space. Both of them got out and checked the back door to make sure it was open. Then they got into the elevator and went down to the casino floor. Vic took the stairs back up to the third level to observe the delivery from a distance, and then call Hank in the casino when it arrived. Moments later, a big SUV drove up and parked next to their van. Things went exactly as planned. A man stepped out of the SUV, looked around, went to the back of the vehicles, opened the back doors on both, and started to transfer the boxes marked "shampoo."

Suddenly, the elevator door opened, and Hank stepped out sporting big sunglasses and a hooded sweatshirt. He went to the passenger side to put the bag and the cell phone on the front seat. Then he sat down in the driver's seat of the rented van. As soon as the transfer was complete, Hank started the van and drove off. Meanwhile, Vic took the stairs to the second level, where Hank would pick him up on the way down.

Arriving on the second level, Vic jumped in, and off they went to the rear lot at the MGM Grand. Hank noticed that Vic was soaking wet, so he asked, "Did the fire sprinklers go off on you?"

"No. You know damn well that my adrenaline together with high blood pressure makes me sweat so much it looks like I stood in the shower with my clothes on. I'm not cut out for this much excitement."

Hank said, " Go up to the room and jump in the shower and put some dry clothes on before you take the van back. In the meantime I'll transfer the shampoo."

"Okay I'll be back in about fifteen minutes. Then I can follow you to drop the van off."

"Might as well grab our stuff and bring it with you when you come back. I don't want to leave the car out of sight." Hank transferred the shampoo (money} and made the phone call to the driver in the van that delivered the goods and is on his way to Hoover Dam.to instruct him what to do.

On the way home they opened several boxes to check content and made plans on how to handle the money, knowing that it couldn't be reported as income. Storage for the money was another problem. They proposed digging a wine cellar with a hidden vault under the house on Hank's farm. This way it would be easily accessible when needed.

Arriving at home, they unloaded the Suburban into Hank's house, into one of the bedrooms, and locked it. His foreman Diego asked Hank, "What were you smuggling?"

Hank said, "Its stuff for the new house. I want to surprise Mary."Hank sent Diego and one other man to take the SUV back to Hertz. After the men left to take the Suburban back Vic and Hank checked some boxes. It seems to be all there.

Then they had to check out the trainees at Vic's place, worked with them for a few hours, and instructed them again about the strict rules that had to be followed, threatening that if they adhered to the rules it would be a pleasant stay, but if not, it could lead to death. Hank said, "Your boss told us if you don't cooperate, we have his permission to do as we please. I have a boss who is a sadist, and he would be pleased to punish you."

In the late afternoon, they went back to Hank's house. Vic was going to take the cashier's check to the escrow company in the morning. They opened all the boxes to check one more time. Everything was in order. Hank suggested that they take one hundred thousand dollars each and give it to the wives to fix up their new houses. Vic agreed. They counted it out and then went to their new homes in Palm Desert. The ladies were still working to get their houses in order. The windfall of money was a dream come true that made it possible for them to buy all the beautiful things that they saw on their shopping trips.

Nancy's bookstore was complete. She planned to have the grand opening in three weeks, well in time for the start of the schools and upcoming tourist season.

The gardeners were starting to replace the flowers, seed the winter grass, and spruce up the art in the median strip of El Paseo. Soon one would see cars from almost every state of the union, Canada, and Mexico. Golf and tennis tournaments would be everywhere. People from around the globe would enjoy winter in the desert, while at home winter storms and frigid temperatures would make life miserable. The majority of the people are from cold climates and are called *snowbirds* or *Frostys*. Northwest seasonal visitors from British Colombia, Washington State, and Oregon are the *rainbirds*. Sometimes local people call them *sprinklers*.

The opening of the bookstore went very well. Nancy was pleased that so many people were interested in books of years gone by. Her specialty is known up and down the West Coast. A few blocks away is the campus of the College of the Desert, also the Eisenhower Medical Center and the Betty Ford Clinic, all potential customers. Nancy was very pleased that some of her old customers from San Francisco showed up. Everyone was impressed with the elegant, sophisticated look of the store.

The men were busy with the trainees. The work was detailed and intense. In addition, they had to deal with the stress of monitoring the two men and the surroundings twenty-four-seven.

As far as the training, there wasn't much to it, except it couldn't be forced. The birds behave a certain way. You can't rush or change the process in any way to make it easier on yourself. You have to go by what they are used to. Otherwise, it creates chaos. After almost ten days, these trainees were ready for their first delivery. They numbered all the pigeons and geese that were to follow the pigeons. Then they loaded the regular poultry for delivery to Carlos. Everything was recorded and photographed to see who was coming and going. Hank made a lot of pictures himself, in case there was a problem later on.

The delivery went smoothly. On the way to the orchard, Hank explained everything to the trainees. With seriousness, he showed them in great detail how to package the cargo and attach it to their legs, then let the trainees try it. Then they took them out into the middle of the yard. Hank showed them how to release them all at the same time. Even that went smoothly. The birds make their usual circles, flew out of sight, and started on their way home. It was a good trip with no problems.

This routine went on for several weeks to perfect the men's performance while the birds got used to them. Finally, after three weeks of training, they got ready for their final trial run. While Hank took them on the trip to watch their performance, Vic removed all the cameras and listening devices. Escrow closed a few days before, so they excitedly anticipated their freedom from this stressful activity, and the pleasant participation in their families' lives.

Hank and the two men came back around noon. Vic asked right away if everything went all right, and Hank told him it had been okay, there was no problem. "The only change I noticed is to let the geese out first so they can see the pigeons before they take off. They should be let out at least a minute or two earlier so they get acclimatized, because the pigeons are so eager to go home,

"Another thing I was thinking about ..."

"What's that?" Vic interrupted. "I can't take these surprises. You're killing me, and my heart can't take this."

"No, it's nothing that concerns us. Since everything with these people is going as planned, I see no reason why I shouldn't tell them they could install a brood-house on the ranch in Mexico, and do the same thing as they are doing over here. The birds from the other side could be brought here on the return trip and fly back to deliver the cash, saving money, and eliminating both the chance of getting caught, and more importantly, people who could spill the beans. I'll type it up in detail and send the suggestion along with the instructions. It might keep them happier and make the deal a little more attractive."

"I'm relieved," said Vic. "I'm still recuperating from Las Vegas, suffering from occasional nightmares."

"Relax," said Hank. "Now we can concentrate on our families and other obligations."

Vic said, "The first thing we have to do is secure the money. We need to build a safe place." Hank had suggested extending his guesthouse with a basement, as they discussed previously.

Hank said, "But I think your property is bigger, and you don't have a guesthouse, so we should build it there."

Vic said, "Let's build one on each property and divide the money. That way we can spend it independently any way we like."

"That's the right way to do it," said Hank. "You're a lot smarter then you look."

"Shut up, Speedy," Vic answered, "That was your title first," referring to their adventures at the Salton Sea. "But you, Hank, are the true and deserving champ."

Hank said, "While I'm taking care of transferring the property, you should get started with plans to do the building for your guesthouse and the addition on my guesthouse. I'll call the guy that built our houses at the ranch. He has his office in El Centro. I'll call him tonight and give them your phone number so he can call you and make an appointment.

"I'm going to meet with Francisco and hand deliver the papers and suggestions to him. I think after that, we're done. The excitement is winding down. I talked to my brother last night, and Jack agreed to have Diego run our place, so I don't have to deal with it anymore. We'll take the Dobermans there. Diego will take care of them.

"My brother also told me that he and Andrea have moved in together in Brentwood. They're also thinking about getting married soon. Andrea mentioned that she would like to get married at the same Little Brown Church in Studio City. The place seems so down-to-earth that she fell in love with it. The girls are really going to be happy to hear that—all three friends from college getting married in the same year and in the same church; it's fantastic. I told Jack that we're happy for him and Andrea, and congratulated him. He seems to be very happy lately. I remember how timid he sounded when he was engaged to Amelia."

"Yeah, I remember," said Vic. "When she took off from here, she left him high and dry. She's a bit of a snob."

"Yes, I guess you're right. That was a little bit too much country for her."

The next morning the meeting with Francisco went well. His bosses seemed to be very happy with the capacity and the security of their new delivery system. "Well, I'm glad it's working out for you guys and you're able to recoup your money very quickly. As far as the real estate you bought, it's actually a very good investment. I think it worked out quite well for both sides."

"I think so too," said Francisco. "I'm sorry about that little misunderstanding. I still consider you my friend."

Hank said, "I hope we stay friends forever. My bosses are also happy with the deal. Good-bye, Francisco."

"Adios amigo," said the fat man, and Hank went out the door.

Hank was very careful and suspicious. He never really trusted Francisco after that incident. On his way home he stopped by at the ranch again to see if everything was okay. There were three more new people working there.

When he arrived home, Hank told Mary about Jack and Andrea's wedding plans. Mary said, "I'm so happy for both of them, and I told her so when she called me yesterday."

"I guess with news like that I'll never get ahead of the girls. I'm happy for them," said Hank, and then he told her about the extension on the guesthouse with the wine cellar. She didn't think that they needed one, but told him to go ahead if it made him happy.

"Victor and Nancy are going to build one, too. We both got interested in buying some rare expensive wines for investments. So we'll need the storage and besides, it's tax deductible."

Hank asked, "How is Henry doing in school?"

Mary said, "It seems so strange to hear you call him Henry."

"I thought we all agreed to untangle the confusion with our names."

"Yes I know. It will take time for me to get used to it. He's doing great. Henry and his friend Jonathan signed up for soccer today."

"That's great. Where is he?"

"He's at Jonathan's house practicing and playing soccer."

"I'm happy he found a friend and shows an interest in sports. It's good for the boy."

With nothing much else to do but supervise, the building of their wine cellars progressed quite rapidly. After the underground concrete work was completed, they started construction of the game room, and Hank's new office. The same contractor did Vic's construction simultaneously, so they guessed they would probably finish at the same time. After six more weeks, both projects were complete. Hank and Vic split and transferred the money. Vic finally could relax.

By then, the winter season in the desert was in full swing. Traffic in the bookstore was picking up. Nancy needed some assistance, so she asked Mary to help. The ladies were quite busy, especially on the weekends.

Hank and Vic spent a lot of time with Henry, going to his soccer practice and games, and taking him and his friend Jonathan fishing at Lake Cahuilla.

Christmas approached, and El Paseo appeared in its breathtaking glory, all dressed up for the holidays. It seemed so magical, with all the beauty and gently caressing desert air, dazzling the people from colder climatic regions. The greens on the golf courses were like fine woven silk in a very special green. Flowers bloomed everywhere, sometimes outdone by bougainvilleas in brilliant purple, red, and white. Swaying palm trees welcomed everyone with a gentle nod. No wonder people flock to this desert paradise. And the nightlife buzzed with clubs and casinos from Palm Springs, Cathedral City, Rancho Mirage, Palm Desert, Indian Wells, La Quinta, and Indio, all along highway 111 and interstate 10.

Hank and Henry were bonding in many ways. There was the father and son relationship, also teacher and student, and a developing friendship between provider, protector, mentor, and dependent. They were very fond of each other.

For his winter holiday, Henry decided to visit his grandparents in Ventura. Mary drove him to her parents' house and returned the same day so she could finish preparation for Christmas. Grandpa and Henry went fishing for two days. After a few days, Henry and his grandparents came back to the desert again for Christmas. In addition, Andrea, Jack, Vic, and Nancy all came to Mary and Hank's house for Christmas. Mary, with help from Nancy, did an amazing job decorating the house inside and outside. It became a Christmas that will be remembered by all the people that were present.

Hank and Vic got to show off their new wine cellars and man-cave-slash-offices. Jack and Andrea announced their wedding day for March 15 at the same church in Studio City. Hank commented on the location of the wedding to his brother: "Oh, how creative!"

Everyone laughed. Even Mr. Hamilton remarked, "We should be able to find that place."

Between Christmas and New Year, Hank, Mary, and Henry suggested a ski trip to Big Bear. Jack recommended Lake Tahoe, and Andrea volunteered to check on snow conditions at different resorts. She learned that Mammoth Mountain had the best snow conditions, so they booked four days at the Austria Hof. Henry was very excited, not knowing what to expect, since he had never seen snow. And of course the idea of snowboarding appealed to him too. He asked if he could bring Jonathan. Hank nodded, "Of course you can." Henry ran out the door, and off he went to Jonathan's house.

Vic stood up and announced some good news: "Nancy and I are expecting a child." Hank jumped up and proposed a toast to the wonderful news. Then Jack proposed a toast to the health of the baby and mother, and the happiness of their little family and circle of friends.

After New Year's Day, things went back to normal. Jack and Andrea went back to Brentwood, the Hamilton's went back to Ventura, and Henry went back to school. When March 15 rolled around, that same group of people assembled at the Little Brown Church in Studio City. The reception was held at Jack and Andrea's house. The house had a totally different feel to it since the last time they saw it. It conveyed a cozy, comfortable feeling—a woman's touch, visible throughout the home.

The following day, the newlyweds went on their honeymoon to Paris. They enjoyed the city and each other for a whole week. As the flight took off for Los Angeles over the city, they promised that they would be back some day, to keep the romance alive.

Life was pretty good by then for the Baldwin brothers. They were both settled down, very happy, and without financial worries to boot.

The years went by in total bliss, as they lived the dream. Henry grew up in a privileged environment. It showed in his behavior, as he was a little bit lazy in his second year at College of the Desert. There was always a party somewhere to go to, and it looked like Henry never missed a single one. The uncanny likeness of his behavior to his father's at this particular age is best described as mind-blowing. His grades suffered, which became a big concern of his parents. Two of his teammates were arrested for using and selling drugs. Two years earlier, the assistant coach and two people on the coaching staff were busted for selling and using cocaine.

Their carefree and wonderful life was turning into a nightmare. Hank and Victor lived with guilt every day, and wore heavily on both of them.

When Vic's daughter was nine years old there were some reports that children in the area as young as eight were being approached by drug peddlers.

Then one Sunday morning, two Sheriff Deputies came to the door and brought the dreadful news that Hank and Mary's son died of an overdose at a drug party by the Salton Sea. Hank and Mary took it very hard. It seemed like their life was unraveling, as Mary descended into deep depression, suffering greatly. After three months, she ended her life with a bottle of sleeping pills.

Hank started drinking again, and he became determined to destroy what he created. When he drove by Vic's old place, he noted that it was like a fort. There was very little he could do to destroy it.

He decided to get to the mountain pass to see if he could stop the birds from delivering their deadly cargo. He bought an all-terrain vehicle and supplies and went into the Chocolate Mountains. These mountains are between their Mexican orchard and the Imperial Valley. Hank's first encounter was with a flock that was on its way to Mexico. He shot two geese, and each one had four thousand dollars on its legs.

So Hank came up with another plan. He thought he would talk to the undesirables in the valley and activate their greed for money and hunger for drugs.

If he could create the figurative perfect storm, it might help him in his quest to erase the horrible mistake he made ten years ago. His wheels were turning. He realized that timing and synchronization were of supreme importance. He came up with a plan to get these drunkards and dope users up the mountains with shotguns, so they could collect their bounty and tell as many of their fellow lowlifes, how easy it is to get money and drugs.

Then he would alert the cartel to the activities and locations. Finally, he'd alert law enforcement to arrange a surprise for the cartel when they show up to surprise the intruders. He'd tell the police, Sheriff, Border Patrol, ATF, FBI marshals and Homeland Security. Everything had to be written out very precisely; especially locations and times, so there would be no time for escapes. And of course, the same thing needed to happen on the Mexican side at the same time.

The only person Hank confided in was Vic. Just hearing Hank's plan was stressful for him. He told Hank, "No matter, if you need help I'll help you; we can do it together."

Hank replied, "No need for your help. Our friendship is solid and true, and there's no need for both of us to take risks. Your daughter and Nancy need you. I'm expendable; my family is destroyed, and it was entirely my fault. You were right, Vic, it was all a stupid idea. I was too stubborn to let it fail and too proud to give up. I would trade it in a minute to turn the clock back ten years. The good times we had when we got married, and even before, that peaceful life in the country, that wonderful life in Palm Desert. The children growing up, the soccer games, the parties, and all our friends. Of course, it's too late for all this reminiscing and feeling sorry for ourselves. That's why I want to redeem myself by destroying as much as I can of these people and their destructive lifestyles. I hope I can pull it off in a big way. Nothing else will relieve my sorrow and self-pity."

To coordinate and synchronize the trap, it would require a healthy respect for devious and clear thinking. Since so many people were involved, to anticipate a completely smooth operation would be unrealistic. But if anyone could do it, Hank was the man.

First, he purchased a half dozen cell phones from different sellers and providers in different names. Using so many different numbers would make tracing his calls more difficult. After that, he would cruise the bars and local hangouts for pimps, prostitutes, and other drug users and pushers. He bought drinks and flaunted money around, letting everybody know where they could get it, and warning each group not to tell anyone else, so they could have it all to themselves. He told them that he knew the next time they would have the chance to score, and that the opportunity occurs every month on the first Tuesday. So without much fanfare, these slime buckets moved up the mountains and camped out with shotguns, ready to claim their anticipated windfall.

That gave Hank almost a month to line things up. Since there were several different groups, they almost started the war too soon, as they were lying to each other about the purpose of their camping on the mountains.

Hank informed cartel about these raiders on the mountains, and they sent an army of gunmen to that lofty location. To alert all the different authorities in California took a while, as he had a hard time explaining exactly the location of the surprise party. For the Mexican side, Hank made a recording in Spanish with a young woman from his staff. He played it on the phone for the Mexican authorities.

After everyone was alerted, Hank loaded his motorcycle on his pickup and drove across the border into Mexicali. He went to the bank and took out as much money with his Visa as they allowed, establishing his presence in Mexicali. He parked his truck on a street not far from the cantina and left his wallet lying on the floorboard. He took his knife and made a small cut in his arm and dripped and smeared the blood all over the cab and door. He patched up his wound, and before he took off, he lit a can of Instant Heat—used to fuel camping stoves—and put it under the seat of his truck, then jumped on his motorcycle and headed for home. Then Hank picked up some money from home, so he wouldn't have to use the ATM in case someone tried to trace him. And he told Vic to take care of the house until the excitement blew over.

Hank said, "I'm pretty sure they're going to be looking for me; I mean the cartel, and maybe some local lowlife who might have gotten away from the surprise party. The law won't look for me; there's nothing illegal about reporting a crime. I can't tell you where I'm going to be, since I don't know myself. I've been in touch with Miranda in Pasadena, and maybe I'll stay there for a while. My name for now is Henry Foster, and I'll get a new cell phone using that name. Then I'll call you and let you know where I am and so on. Give your girls my love, and explain to Nancy what had to be done."

He took off with a heavy heart. As he was leaving, he turned around and told Vic, "Tell my brother and Andrea that I'm okay and that I have to lay low for a while."

He stopped at a Holiday Inn in San Bernardino to watch the news and see what was happening. There was no news about the Imperial Valley or drugs, or arrests of drug users—nothing at all. Hank was very depressed until he fell asleep.

He had slept for about three hours when a louder-than-usual bulletin came on the television reporting on a turf war in the Chocolate Mountains above Imperial Valley. The government agencies involved, including the FBI; Homeland Security; Sheriff; and Bureau of Alcohol, Tobacco, Firearms and Explosives lost two people to injuries, one FBI agent got shot in the arm, and the Border Patrol had two injuries reported. Twelve people were killed who belonged to a drug cartel. Seven people were found shot to death in their tents, said to be campers. One helicopter had to make an emergency landing upon receiving heavy gunfire. Hank felt bad about the injuries of law enforcement, but overall he was pleased. The next morning, they also reported a similar situation on the Mexican side with fourteen people from the cartel dead and one police officer in critical condition. On the California side, they were still chasing more gunmen from the cartel that fled the scene throughout the mountainous region.

Hank called Miranda to let her know that he was coming to see her. He asked her if he could stay for a few days, and she said of course he could come and stay as long as he liked. Since her mother passed away, she has had an extra bedroom, so space was no problem. He thanked her and told her that he would be there in about an hour, if traffic permitted. They had seen each other only four or five times in the last ten years. So neither one of them knew what to expect.

Hank showed up about eleven o'clock. Both of them were really happy to see each other. Miranda already had the table set for lunch. They had so much catching up to do that they completely forgot about that lunch. After about an hour Miranda excused herself and told Hank that she had to go to work for a couple of hours. They hired two new people, and she had to see how they were doing, and would be back about four thirty.

"Do you want me to bring anything from the store?" asked Miranda.

"No thank you, I think I'm okay for now."

Hank settled down for the afternoon on the living room couch to watch some more news. The big news of the day, of course, was about the drug wars in the Imperial Valley and surrounding areas. This turned out to be a big deal, and better than expected. He fell into a peaceful sleep until Miranda came home with dinner. They had a lovely evening on Memory Lane till late into the night. Miranda, of course, knew all about the misfortunes that consumed Hank's life the last couple of years. He was obsessed with somehow taking revenge and making things right. Miranda thought that he accomplished that, and Hank felt totally at peace within himself.

The next day, the two of them went shopping for a new cell phone for his new "Henry Foster" identity. As soon as they came home,

Hank called Vic and asked if there had been any suspicious activity anywhere around the house or the neighborhood. Vic, of course, being himself, was happy to report that nothing was happening. He said in a deep voice, "Nothing to report, Mr. Foster."

Hank said, "You can't be too careful; these people are brutal. If they suspect me as the stool pigeon, you can bet that they will be looking for me. To ease my mind, I just tell myself that the law isn't looking for me."

Vic said, "Did you see some of the firefights with grenades and shoulder-fired missiles? It looked like a war movie that Spielberg came up with. There's going to be a special tomorrow on television. Some call it the border wars, others call it drug wars, and you, of course, called it a surprise party. Hank, every news organization in the country and from around the world is in this Valley. I'm telling you, this is huge. And yesterday on the news, I saw some clips from Mexicali. I'm pretty sure the cartel found your truck. I saw the burned-out shell, but the last four numbers on your plates were visible. So they're not going to be looking for you if they think you're dead. I'll keep my eyes open and will inform you, Mr. Foster."

"Very funny," said Hank, "and thank you. I see your sense of humor is still intact. If anything comes up, you have my number. Call me so I can react accordingly. Take care, and give my love to the girls."

Hank stayed at Miranda's for six weeks, and they became an item. Hank convinced her to quit her job and move in with him in Palm Desert, which she did.

They lived together in a relatively peaceful environment, until a young man showed up in a stretch limo at their door and asked for Mr. Hank Baldwin. When Hank answered the door, the man punched him in the face and told him, "I promised my mother to deliver this before she passed on. Her name was Pat Wilson and my name is Hank."